THE ANTIGUA TRAIL

Book two of the Undisturbed Islands Trilogy

J WILLIAM

For my family, friends, and beautiful fiancée

Dear Reader,

Some of you may find the spelling is not what you are used to. The story is written using British English, and has characters who are American, Australian, and British, and as such, their thoughts and speaking parts will be in their native language; which might not be words you are familiar with, but they are not errors. I hope you enjoy the variety.

Table of Contents

CHAPTER 1: THE SHIP

Jonas Sands stared into the burning oil lamp on his desk, his eyes following the trail of light as it rose and fell in tandem with the ship, gently bobbing up and down on the waves.

The water was relatively calm outside his cabin and up on deck was as peaceful as it could be, but it wouldn't stay that way for long. A violent storm was coming, he could feel it.

He went over his dilemma again trying to think of another way, but deep down he knew there was only one solution.

They must never be found.

He thought back to when they had first arrived, all those years ago. He had been so damn confident they had no way of escaping he'd taken an age to set up his patrols. When he'd first heard they might have a runaway he couldn't—wouldn't—believe it. Shock turned to anger, first blaming himself then his men, but none of it brought the runaway back. Instead, his trail went cold.

The only positive was that it hadn't been *him*. *He* would have come straight for Jonas's throat, but Captain Sands hadn't found much solace there. They had a leak, and that meant one day the lot of them could be set free, he just didn't know when. He almost wished it had been *him*, at least then the whole thing would have been resolved swiftly. Instead, he just had to wait, second-guessing the runaway's every move, and enduring the daily torment of wondering if today, might finally be the day he returns.

As soon as he had been certain one of the prisoners had indeed made it off the island alive he'd used his substantial resources to try and hunt him down, but other than one initial sighting there had been nothing.

He'd interrogated his unfortunate lookout, far beyond what most of the men were comfortable with, but it hadn't done much good. After the man had spilled every last drop of information, and a disproportionate amount of his blood, Jonas confirmed only what he'd already known; a prisoner had escaped and made it to the mainland, and that meant one day someone would come looking—which was a big problem.

Jonas hauled himself upright. He placed his large weathered hands on the heavy wooden desk in front of him, hung his head and shut his eyes.

He could see the beach where they'd dumped the prisoners on the sand bound and gagged, before pulling off their blindfolds one by one. He'd looked into each of their eyes in turn as they'd suppressed sobs and screams, kneeling or lying on the shore, attempting to maintain their pride but all utterly ruined. He'd found only surrender from those still breathing—except *him.*

Unbearably, their captain had stared wild-eyed at Jonas like a crazed animal, conveying his promise to tear him limb from limb should he ever get free, without needing to say a word.

He had known then he should have tied up the loose ends. Ended it to make sure. But *they* hadn't allowed it. If he'd wanted the deal to go through then their captain's life had been an unbreakable condition. And he'd wanted the deal more than anything.

It still maddened him that this man had shown no regard for him, no fear, not even facing death. Jonas had looked harder at him than any of the others, trying to break him, but whatever darkness lay behind those eyes had been too much even for Jonas, and it had almost forced him to look away—almost.

His own rage had been so bitter he would rather have died then and there than flinch and lose face, again. It had taken a monumental effort to stop himself emptying the captain's blood at his feet. But somehow he'd stayed his hand and completed the task that had needed to be carried out in order for the plan to work.

The outcome had been almost perfect. He'd gotten what he wanted, and the bastard and his pathetic crew of traitors got theirs, there was no way they were ever getting out of there.

Yet one of them had, and they'd made it to the mainland. Beyond that he dreaded to think; except he did think about it, relentlessly.

The runaway had haunted his thoughts for what felt like an eternity.

It had all happened so long ago, and for so many years they'd just carried on. Most of the men had all but forgotten the runaway, but Jonas was obsessed, and now he could feel the thread that had loosened was finally unravelling, and everything he'd feared most was starting to happen.

He opened his eyes and ran his big fingers through his thinning brown hair. He paced across the wooden boards of his cabin and, for the first time, he began to think that his past failure might really be the end of him.

Jonas slammed both fists down on his desk, the noise echoing around his chamber.

NO!

He gripped the neck of the open wine bottle that had been sitting next to his oil lamp, tipped his head back, and gulped down three large mouthfuls.

All those years ago he'd taken a huge roll of the dice to secure his position at the top of the food chain, and for the first time since he'd gambled, and won, he was afraid.

But he wasn't going to sacrifice everything he'd worked so hard to accomplish without a fight.

He straightened himself up to his full and considerable height, and pushed all thoughts of the escapee, the captain on the beach, and the limitless spiteful possibilities that he imagined were coming for him from his head.

"They'll stay buried. I'll make damn sure of it," he spat, clenching his fists as he strode for the door.

CHAPTER 2: THE PLANE

"Well, here we are again," Amy said, turning to look at Billy in the window seat to her right and grinning.

Her bright orange lipstick lit up her face.

"Uh huh, feels like a long time ago since our last flight," Billy replied.

She turned back to the tiny screen in front of her, put her headphones on and began flicking through the movies.

Issy's nose poked through the gap of the two seats in front.

"Ames, what are you going to watch?" she loudly whispered to her friend sitting behind her.

"Not sure, looking now," Amy replied even louder, her headphones still on.

Issy studied Amy's face for a few seconds, before turning back around and returning to her conversation with Jake, who sat next to her.

To anyone else on the plane they looked like a perfectly normal group of twenty-somethings excited about their holiday.

But Billy had seen Issy's concern, she'd turned around three times in the last five minutes, and he knew she was worried.

Billy hadn't been fooled by Amy's full bright lips either, at least, not for long he hadn't. He'd scanned her features for signs of—he wasn't sure what—and found dark rings beneath her even darker pupils.

It was no surprise she was still suffering, after what they'd been through. They all were, but Amy worst of all.

Fragmented memories of all that had happened since they'd met just a week ago flooded his mind and he had to shut his eyes to stem the flow.

He couldn't allow it all in. Not now, he wasn't ready, and they had work to do.

"Let's get some drinks, shall we?" Amy stated, pouncing on Billy and making him jump. Obviously, no movie had taken her fancy.

He hesitated. On their first flight together Billy and Amy had swapped seats with Jake and Issy, and they'd ended up getting tipsy together.

But it was different now. Billy still fancied her; he loved her directness, her style, her Australian accent, and it was hard not to notice her slender thighs and significant curves given they were normally accentuated by her choice of outfits. He'd even seen her in nothing but her underwear one stormy night less than a week ago. The evening definitely had not gone to plan, but her figure was still emblazoned on his memory.

Now though, there was more to it than hoping she'd want to jump into bed with him, although that was something he couldn't help thinking about. He was worried about her, and he felt a bit protective too—but there was something else.

He chased the thought around his head until finally he caught it, pushing it back as soon as he realised what it was.

It was fear—Billy was afraid of her.

She was much better now than *that* night in his room, but something was still out of place.

Not all the time, just sometimes. Her patience was shorter, and once or twice she'd been quick to anger and had given him a look that had made him wither.

In those moments, Amy hadn't been anywhere to be found and it had felt to Billy like he was looking at someone else entirely.

CHAPTER 3: THE ISLAND

The Ghost surveyed the same view he'd been surveying for… he couldn't remember.

Right in front of him were row upon row of palm trees. He'd stared at them for so long he swore he'd actually watched them grow before his eyes.

In the same direction he was facing he could still make out a faint rainforest path leading away from him towards the shore.

Beyond that he could just catch a glimpse of the emerald blue water in the distance, lapping at the white sand beach he'd been so unceremoniously dumped on.

His pseudonym had never felt more fitting.

His first crew had nicknamed him the Ghost after they'd taken their maiden ship by surprise, capturing and ransacking the vessel with the minimum of fuss.

Thomas had planned and led the assault, preaching beforehand to his men the benefit of taking their enemy unaware, and leaving without a trace so they could never be caught. He'd gone over the plan with them a dozen times, unrelenting even when he knew they were getting restless and just wanted to get on with it.

His methods had been extremely successful.

Afterwards, when they were safely on their way, the men had been in awe of Thomas and had bestowed *the Ghost* nickname upon him. Some of them for his ability to make himself appear and disappear like an apparition, others because they were just plain scared of him.

Part of the reason the plan had gone so well was because Thomas had been so unwavering and ruthless once the attack had begun. The sight of him striding across the deck, eyes focussed and emotionless, cutting down anyone who stood in his way was enough to send many of the enemy crew overboard on its own.

He was a disturbing figure even when he was at rest, with short-cropped dark brown hair pushed back across his skull, a rough-hewn wood-coloured beard, and brown eyes so dark they were practically black. He had a brawler's body, scarred and muscular, which was easy to see through the loose shirts he wore open at the chest and wrists that normally carried a combination of mud, sweat, and blood stains on them. He wasn't one for jokes or banter, kept himself to himself, and had an animalistic quality that caused even the more battle and sea-hardened sailors to give him a wider berth than they otherwise would have.

Over the years his crew changed, and the story of *the Ghost* evolved and got retold, and retold, before eventually truth was lost, and myth took over. The Ghost became a demonic monster of a man, who razed entire fleets in the dead of night, almost single-handed.

Thomas never recognised himself in the tales to begin with, and even less so as they became more far-fetched. He didn't spare them a lot of thought; until he was captured.

He was certain the man who'd caged him had taken particular pleasure in making the infamous *Ghost* live out his own legend, but with a very different twist. Time, and life, passing right past him, his existence nothing more than a fading memory, no longer real nor able to influence anything around him.

Sometimes he wasn't sure if he was even still alive at all, such was the job his captor had done on him.

Today, however, he felt, *different.*

He'd been feeling more *present* recently, and he was almost certain he knew why.

Nothing had changed as far as he could see. The palm leaves were still right in front of him, heavy with water today, buckling under the weight of the rain as it hammered down. And the rainforest path and unreachable waters beyond were as vivid as always.

But he could see something else too. Intermittently, it hovered over the top of what was normally there, obscuring his view.

17

Right now, he was looking at blue sky and clouds out of a tiny porthole—and then people, sat in a row.

It's them. They're coming.

He strained his mind to try and see clearer, but the vision vanished.

Thomas had seen similar visions before. He strained to recollect whether they'd been in the last few days, or weeks, or maybe even months. He wasn't sure when and it maddened him that he couldn't be more precise. He found it hard to place time, stuck where he was.

But he was certain they were becoming more frequent, and stronger.

Excitement grew like a fever inside him.

They're coming.

He tried desperately to block out every sight and smell from the island, concentrating as hard as he could on drawing them nearer.

CHAPTER 4: LANDING

It was only a short hop over from Grantley Adams to V. C. Bird International Airport, and the plane had already begun its descent before any of them had really had a chance to settle.

"It looks beautiful," Amy said, leaning completely over Billy and admiring the bright white slivers of beach clinging to the coastline and the lush greens further inland.

She moved herself closer to the tiny window trying to get her bearings, her chest pressing against Billy's abdomen, leaving him trapped and unsure of what to do with his hands.

"We're staying on the south west side of the island…" he said, trying to break the silence and drag his mind away from their bodies now firmly squashed together. "So, we need to go top to bottom." He cursed himself as soon as the words escaped his lips, and prayed Amy didn't think he was attempting a line.

"It's about a half hour drive, I think," he added quickly. "We should get a good first look at the island on the way."

* * *

Amy sat back in her seat completely unaware of how awkward she was making him feel.

She smiled to herself thinking about what they were going to eat when they arrived at their guest house and wondered if it had a pool. She'd brought five different swimsuits with her to Barbados but, following the traumatic events on that island, she'd only been able to wear one so far. She really hoped Antigua would be different.

* * *

Billy watched her daydreaming and relaxed. He'd escaped without embarrassment, and she was herself again, for now.

CHAPTER 5: TAXI

The journey across the island had been a stressful one for Issy.

She was still worried about Amy, and she had an inescapable sense they were in danger, again.

As their taxi wove along the sun-beaten dusty roads she'd been scouring the streets and staring intently at the treeline to see something, but she didn't know what.

She'd frequently turned around to check if anyone was behind them, and she'd sworn she'd seen the same black pick-up truck more than once. But just as she'd thought she'd caught another glimpse, she also noticed Amy looking at her, worried, and she'd stopped. She hadn't looked around since, instead trying to focus on the driver's wing mirror to see if she could spot any pursuer that way.

As the car pulled along Old Road with Mount Obama now ahead and on their right, Issy saw the sea properly for the first time, distracted from her duties as protector.

If this is the last place I see it could be worse, I guess. She was mesmerised by the dark, foam-capped blues and aqua greens flickering in the sunlight.

The taxi jolted left on to a narrow side road which wound down towards the water. After a few more minutes they'd all but left civilisation behind, with only rainforest, beach, and bright shining sea around them, and not another person in sight.

The dirt road kept winding and finally spat them out in a small secluded bay. Aside from a fisherman perched on a rock, they were completely alone. There were no bars or guest houses or hotels along the beach. No sunbathers, no surfers, no people swimming or splashing in the shallow water. The place was eerily quiet.

"Where are we?" Jake asked, staring hard out the car window, stunned by his new surroundings. "How did you find this place?"

"I thought it would be better this time if, you know, there were less people around." Billy shrugged.

"I mean, yeh, I agree, but where are we even going? Are there *any* people around? I can't even see one house," Jake stated, mock complaining but clearly delighted they had an idyllic stretch of sand, fringed with palm trees, all to themselves.

"It should be a bit further up... Yeh, there it is. See that bit of jungle up ahead?"

The others nodded.

"You see where the road disappears into it?"

They nodded again.

"I think our guest house must be in there," Billy said.

They all stared ahead as the car slowly manoeuvred its way along the ever narrowing road past the deserted shore to their left and made its way towards the dark patch of rainforest.

"This place does have showers, right?" Amy asked after a long silence.

Billy went to answer then stopped, doubting what he'd read about the lodgings he'd booked for them online, and unable to understand how they even had internet.

He looked at their driver for reassurance, but even he looked a little tense.

Billy wanted to ask him how often he'd been down this way, but again stopped himself, fearing he probably wouldn't like the answer.

He looked out his window at the pristine beach with nothing on it but a bit of sea debris and marvelled at how they'd managed to stumble across such a beautiful spot completely free of tourists. Then he saw something move on top of a faded branch nestled in the sand. Stood up on its hind legs, its neck outstretched high in the air, was a light turquoise lizard with darker green stripes on its back.

He watched its head turning in jerky movements as it appeared to scan the horizon.

Billy was about to tell the others when he stopped himself again.

The lizard had leaned down to the side obscured from Billy's view and had picked something up in its mouth. It was darker than the lizard, and whatever it had bitten in to was almost as big as the lizard's entire body.

It flung the dark object on to the sand and threw itself down on top of it, wildly devouring whatever it had captured.

As they continued their journey Billy's viewpoint changed and he could only see its hind legs and tail thrashing around. He had to wait until the car had continued along the road a bit more to get a better angle, and for the creature to come fully back into view again.

When the scene revealed itself in all its gory horror, Billy almost screamed.

Lying in severed bits on the sand was a large turtle. The dark object which had been in the lizard's mouth and was gradually being ripped apart one chunk at a time, was one of the turtle's legs. Its head was barely still attached and lolled unnaturally at the lizard's feet and was at such an angle it looked like it was being forced to watch its attacker consume the rest of its body.

The lizard suddenly stopped, raised itself up on its hind legs once more and turned towards the car, blood dripping from its little jaws.

"*Fuck me*," Billy said quietly, turning away in disgust.

* * *

"You okay?" Amy asked.

Jake and Issy barely noticed his reaction.

She leaned forward and touched Billy's shoulder from the back seat, making him jump.

He turned around to face her as much as his seatbelt would allow.

His face was pale, and even though he'd managed a weak smile, Amy could see he was disturbed. Her first suspicion was their driver, and as she stared at the back of his head, she wondered what he could have done to upset Billy—and if he posed them any threat.

He was a lot older than they were, maybe in his early sixties, and thin. As she continued to stare, beads of sweat appeared from his short black hair at the base of his skull, forming droplets and running down his bony neck and inside his off-white shirt.

Sensing someone was watching him the driver glanced over his shoulder. He caught a glimpse of Amy's eyes, which had turned blacker than night, and snapped his head back in position, instinctively pressing more firmly on the accelerator and speeding the car up.

It's not him.

Amy sat back in her seat. She didn't know where the danger was coming from but she knew there was a threat.

They were out there, and they were looking for them.

Unable to do any more until they arrived, she repositioned herself to get comfortable again, tucked her hair behind her ear, and contemplated their next move.

CHAPTER 6: THE GUEST HOUSE

"Wild Bay Inn," Jake said, reading the sign as he helped the driver lift the last of the bags from the boot of the car. "Well, at least it actually exists."

"It looks kind of… cute," Issy said, searching for something positive to say.

"Yeh, in an abandoned, isolated, 'Scream and no one will hear you,' kind of way," Amy said dryly.

She grabbed the handle of her suitcase in one hand and reached for Issy's hand with the other. "Come on, let's go and see what nightmare these two idiots have dragged us in to this time."

Issy laughed as they walked along the short garden path through the trees up to the front porch in search of a reception.

"They're right. Let's go. The sooner we see our room the sooner we can get over the disappointment," Jake joked.

But when he saw his friend wasn't laughing he added, "Honestly, it doesn't matter what the place is like, that's not why we're here, right? This is a great location to find the next clue."

Billy still hadn't said a word.

"You did great, mate, we're just joking about this place. You okay?"

Billy hadn't really been listening, his mind had been elsewhere. "Yeh, I'm okay. It's not that… I mean, you're right," he said. Jake's words finally registering, "This place is like something from a horror film and considering we're on a tropical paradise island, I'd say I've outdone myself to find a Caribbean version of the Bates Motel."

"So, what's up?" Jake pressed as they stood unmoving on the narrow walkway.

"I don't know, I saw something on the way here. Sounds crazy but it was a lizard tearing a turtle apart on the beach, I mean the thing had this bloodlust and it was going to town and... this is the craziest part, I *swear* it caught me looking at it," Billy said, worrying he was losing his mind.

Most people would have laughed, but Jake listened intently. They'd seen plenty of unusual things on their journey together already, and most of them had either intended or actually caused them harm.

"What do you mean?" Jake asked.

"I know, I know it sounds crazy—" Billy wished he hadn't said anything.

"No, I mean, can you explain in more detail? I didn't think lizards were dangerous, or ate anything that big," Jake said more carefully.

"Neither did I, and this thing wasn't just eating it, it was *enjoying* it. I mean that's what it looked like. And then it was like it sensed I was staring at it and it stopped and looked at me and... I can't explain it, but it gave me the creeps big time."

"We should make sure none of the little fuckers can get in at night, or any other time for that matter. Let's go and see where we're sleeping, and we can try and secure the rooms as best we can. Maybe you can distract the girls while I check their room for them, there's no point freaking them out already. We've only just arrived," Jake said.

Billy nodded, grateful Jake had believed him, and feeling a little better about the whole situation.

Catching up to Issy and Amy at the small front desk, they could both see Amy was agitated.

"I've rung the bell like a hundred times and nothing," she said impatiently.

"Wait here, I'll take a look around and see if I can find someone," Billy said, dropping his bag by their feet.

He realised as he'd said it that his offer sounded slightly ridiculous because of the size of the guest house. There were probably no more than a handful of rooms in the whole property, and the front desk was basically a corner of what appeared to be a communal living room.

They could see the entire downstairs space from where they stood.

"I'll check upstairs then," Billy said sheepishly.

He squeezed past the others and made his way to the winding staircase at the back of the room. Grabbing hold of the banister he carefully placed one boot at a time, making his way upwards, and looking directly ahead so he could see as far as possible in front of him. He really didn't fancy bumping into anyone unsuspectingly. He couldn't handle that right now. The stairwell was a tight squeeze, especially for Billy who was by far the biggest of their group, and the higher he climbed the more claustrophobic and jittery he felt.

When he reached the top, he peered along the landing left and right, remaining on the stairs in case he needed to make a quick escape.

But there was nothing.

He could see three doors down a short corridor to his right, and one door unnervingly close to his face directly to his left. All shut.

The prospect of going and knocking on all the doors to see if anyone answered, and worse, if they didn't answer trying the door handles to see if he could get in, was a daunting one. But he decided there was no point in him coming this far if he was just going to go straight back down. He'd also look like a chicken in front of the others, and he'd probably freak them out as much as himself.

He hauled his big body up on to the landing and decided he'd try the doors to his right first. There was something about the door to his left, the one closest to him, that he really didn't like.

Billy gave each door a short but firm tap. When there was no answer he tried the handle, but no one answered and none of them budged.

He then turned to face the final door which he'd saved until last, hoping he wouldn't have to try that one at all.

One of the floorboards creaked loudly underfoot as he stepped across the landing making him jump.

"Fuck you," he hissed to the building itself, pulling himself together.

Billy knocked on the door. No answer.

He took a deep breath and tried the final door handle, which to his disappointment offered absolutely no resistance. Expecting it to be locked Billy had used the same force as with the other doors and fell straight through, only just managing to stay on his feet. He righted himself quickly and scanned inside.

His first thought was that it looked like the inside of an old ship's cabin. Not that he'd ever seen one, other than in movies, but this was exactly how he'd imagined one would look.

There were scrolls of paper neatly lined up on a big wooden desk, maps covering the wall with markings and scribbled comments dotted across them, and half a dozen dusty chests containing who knows what.

Sunlight spilled from the small window opposite the doorway, with one of the beams shining brightly on a small but distinct map which had been pinned to a board directly above the desk. He took one small step forward and leaned in for a closer look.

The paper the map was drawn on was brown and the markings had faded, not as much as the maps they'd discovered, but he assumed they must still be pretty old.

I hope they're safe. His mind drifting momentarily to the three rum bottles, each with a different map on the label, carefully stowed away in their luggage.

"Looks like... islands," Billy whispered under his breath, panicking. His first thought was that somehow the owner of this guest house had a copy of the very same maps they were carrying, but after a closer inspection he decided that, even though Barbados and Antigua, plus the third island they hadn't yet identified, could well be on there, the focus on this map was on the sea, not the land.

Four, five, six... seven. Billy lost count of the different markings off the coast and could only guess at what they might mean.

"What are you, huh? Shipping routes? Fishing spots? Or something *else*?" he muttered, his brow creasing in concentration.

"HEY! What are you doing up there??" Amy yelled irritably from downstairs, making him jump and break out in a cold sweat. He took a deep breath and tried to calm his heart from pounding quite so hard.

He kept still, staring down the corridor and expecting someone to burst forth from one of the other rooms to confront him. After a minute or two, convinced he was still alone, he shut the door carefully and crept back down the staircase to re-join the others.

He knew he had to tell them everything he'd seen. They'd made a pact to share everything—full disclosure. But they didn't need to know right now. He'd tell them when they were more settled.

"Sorry, nothing up there and all the doors are locked," he lied. "I'll go and check out back."

"Okay, but hurry the hell up, I want a shower, a change of clothes, and some sort of cocktail in my hand within the next half hour," Amy declared.

Billy saw her smile, but knew she was only half joking. He hurried through the communal living area and out through faded yellow French doors onto wooden decking, which was surrounded by so much thick foliage it blocked out most of the Caribbean sun.

As he slowly looked around for the owner he saw a little path leading away into the dark jungle rainforest beyond, and he prayed they wouldn't have to see where it went. Before he could dwell on the path any longer he spotted a man sitting cross-legged on a bench a few feet away, looking at him.

The man had a book in his hand which he'd obviously been reading and was holding his page with his thumb and forefinger, waiting to assess how long Billy's interruption would last before he decided whether to part with the book fully or continue reading.

"Mr. Willis?" asked the stranger with the book.

Billy had forgotten he'd used a fake name when making the booking. He'd figured whoever had been after them in Barbados was probably still looking, and he didn't know how well connected they were. Safer to go with a fake name and Die Hard had been the first thing that had sprung to his mind. But as the stranger waited expectantly, Billy's mind was blank.

It took him an awkward moment to remember what he'd done, which was long enough to raise the stranger's suspicions and, Billy suspected, undo his good work of changing his name in the first place.

"Yes, that's me," he said, when his brain finally caught up with his situation. "And the other three are just inside," he added quickly, motioning behind him towards the lounge area.

"We've just arrived and would like to check in, if that's okay?"

The stranger looked at Billy for a moment longer then nodded. He folded the corner of his page to mark where he was up to and placed the book on the seat next to him. Reaching down to his opposite side he retrieved a half-smoked roll-up cigarette and a black lighter next to it. He lit the end, took a couple of short puffs to get it going, and then a few long drags before he finally got up and walked inside to reception without saying a word.

He was a lot younger than Billy had expected, and not that much older than them. Late twenties maybe, or early thirties. He had medium-length mousy brown hair, a goatee beard, and stubble across the rest of his face

Billy had assumed anyone living in this much isolation must be approaching the end of their life and had decided they didn't want to be a part of the world anymore. But what this guy was doing on a deserted beach running a guest house in the middle of a jungle he had no idea. Then a thought dawned on him.

He's hiding from something.

Billy followed the man inside and joined the others.

Jake was engrossed in a painting on the wall furthest from reception, and Amy and Issy were huddled together on a sofa in the living area deep in conversation, having found a topic interesting enough to distract themselves from their hunger and frustration at not being able to check in yet.

Amy whispered something in Issy's ear, and she burst out laughing, filling the room with the sound. Issy didn't notice the stranger creep in or pad quietly behind the reception counter, but she spotted Billy's big frame almost as soon as he stepped inside and stopped laughing abruptly. She was, however, unable to wipe the broad smile from her face.

He looked at the pair of them trying to look innocent and struggling not to laugh. Amy's dark brown hair had grown ever so slightly since he'd first met her and dropped just below her jawline, one side hanging loose and flicking up at the end towards her impish smile, and the other tucked behind her ear. Issy was pressed up against her, giggling hysterically, her blonde pony-tail dangling over one shoulder.

"Figures. At least they're not mad at me," Billy muttered.

He loved how the pair of them always managed to find something to laugh at despite everything they'd been through, even if, in this case, it was him.

He turned to the receptionist and asked for their room keys. He badly wanted to ask all the questions that had sprung to his mind since they'd first found the place, but he decided they could do that later, after a shower and a nap.

"Just one moment, please," the stranger said, his accent unmistakably Spanish, although faded.

Jake snapped from his trance at the stranger's voice and turned away from the painting to see who the new person was. Issy and Amy did the same, their smiles vanishing.

The eerie quiet of when they'd first arrived returned despite the additional body in the room, and nothing more than a few stolen looks were exchanged between the five of them as the stranger at reception filled out the necessary paperwork.

Billy did ask a few simple questions out of basic courtesy, and to break the awkward silence more than anything. The stranger's name was Nicolas, and he was the manager. He answered politely, and somewhat guardedly, offering nothing up for free.

"Here are your keys. Go on up and I'll bring your bags up for you shortly," he offered.

"No," Jake answered on reflex, thinking of the rum bottles hidden in their bags.

The looks of panic were clearly noted by Nicolas.

"I mean don't worry, we can take them. We don't have a lot of stuff," he added, reddening at his mistake. He'd increased suspicion on their group, the last thing they needed right now.

"As you wish," Nicolas said flatly.

With nothing left to say they gathered their belongings and forced them carefully up the winding staircase in search of their rooms and some privacy, where they could debrief and discuss what they should do next.

"At least no one will find us here. I don't even think I could find the way here again!" Issy whispered to Amy as she turned the key in their door and shuffled inside with her bag.

Amy looked back along the darkening corridor as the light coming through the one tiny window faded with the setting sun.

She waited for Issy to go safely inside before scanning the landing one last time.

"I'm not so sure," she whispered softly.

CHAPTER 7: THE WATCHMAN

He repositioned himself carefully, his chest in the mud, keeping still and silent.

The Watchman waited.

He'd waited for their plane at the airport. He'd followed them at a distance in his black pick-up, and he'd seen them arrive and go inside.

He knew where they were, but still, he waited.

Over the hours that had passed since he'd taken up his position on the hill high above them, only the local wildlife had been aware of his presence. But even the lizards and spiders scuttled away sensing danger when they got too close.

He held his spyglass perfectly stationary and surveyed his target again.

The path leading up to the Wild Bay Inn was relatively exposed, and there were thick trees and creepers nestling either side of the building, making manoeuvrability on either side of the guest house problematic.

The back, however, was interesting.

The Watchman could clearly see a section of the decking where Billy had first met Nicolas. There was plenty of cover at the back, with large and medium-sized trees, creepers, and shrubs to hide behind. There was also the path that led up from the beach, through the jungle, opening out where Billy had been looking earlier.

It would lead him right to them and they wouldn't see or hear a thing until he was within striking range, and then it would be too late.

He needed to make sure, his life probably depended on it.

In the fading light he surveyed the grounds once more.

Something shone brightly and caught his eye to the back of the guest house. The Watchman quickly scanned the area to find the source, but it had gone.

He held his breath keeping his eye fixed on the patch of decking that had attracted his attention.

There it was again.

This time the Watchman was staring directly at the light as it appeared, a tiny dot at first before glowing brighter then disappearing again.

He's smoking.

Now knowing what the light was and where it was coming from the Watchman adjusted his focus.

As darkness closed in he could just make out the angular figure of Nicolas standing sentry-like as though guarding the back entrance. The same entrance the Watchman had decided to use as his point of attack.

Do they know? It's impossible!

The Watchman felt restless for the first time, frustration sparking inside him.

No. It's coincidence. He'll leave and go back inside soon. Wait. Wait.

The Watchman calmed himself, resettled, and waited, keeping his spyglass aimed at the intermittent glow of Nicolas's roll-up cigarette.

Nicolas finished and stubbed the butt out in the small wooden ashtray he'd brought out with him, but he did not return inside.

Maybe twenty minutes passed. Nicolas remained perfectly still staring out into the darkness along the jungle path.

The Watchman watched, and waited, nagging doubt now seeping into his mind.

Why isn't he going?

Nicolas reached into his shirt pocket, gathered his tobacco, rolling papers and filters, and slowly began making another cigarette.

He lit the end and took more short puffs to get it going before inhaling a long, deep drag and slowly exhaling a large cloud of smoke.

He wasn't going anywhere, and the Watchman knew it.

How? Is it just him or do they all know?

The Watchman put away his spyglass and lay a while longer contemplating his next move.

He could still attack now. There was one man on guard, he was certain now he was on guard, but what difference really did that make?

He let the bloody encounter play out in his mind.

What if one of them escapes?

He couldn't risk it. A fight might give one of them warning enough to run and elude him. And that wouldn't do, he needed to make sure.

The Watchman slowly rose to his feet, his decision having been made.

He'd have to remain patient and wait for a better opportunity, one where he could finish them all in one go.

CHAPTER 8: THE SECOND ANCHOR

The next morning they were all gathered in Billy and Jake's room.

"It looks like it's on the edge of that cliff," Jake said, holding aloft one of the rum bottles and pointing at a dark mark on a faded map of Antigua on the bottle's label.

In the southwest corner of the island, above some jagged lines that looked like a rocky outcrop or cliff face, was a compass, more prominent than the other markings, like it had been drawn over more than once.

"I know," said Billy. He was frustrated. They had all assumed that once they arrived in Antigua, the rum bottle map would lead them to the next clue. They'd overlooked the fact the map was probably around three hundred years old, had faded to hell, and didn't give an exact location of where they were supposed to go.

"Well, how are we going to get up there?" Jake asked. "There's no road or path, according to Google maps. How are we going to find this thing?"

"I don't fucking know!" Billy said through gritted teeth, running his hand roughly through his short wavy black hair.

"Keep it down, we don't need any more attention right now," Amy said, touching Billy's shoulder. "We don't know a thing about Nicolas—and he's weird."

Billy remembered the room he'd entered yesterday and didn't mention, and wished he'd told them sooner. He decided now was as good a time as any.

"He's... afraid of something. Someone. Maybe the same guy who was chasing us in Barbados."

"How do you know?" Issy asked.

"I don't... know. But, when I was looking for him when we arrived, one of the doors was unlocked upstairs. I think it was his room."

He paused, waiting to be chastised for not telling them sooner.

"And?" Amy demanded impatiently.

"It was like a ship's cabin, covered in maps, charts, and who knows what. Anyways, I had a quick look at some of the maps, the ones which had the most markings and looked the most used."

He caught Jake's expression. "Don't worry, they're not the same as our maps… although both Barbados and Antigua were on there, and a bunch of other islands.

"But the focus wasn't inland, it was on the sea. There were dozens of markings, with notes underneath. I couldn't understand the writing and I only had a quick glance. I think now it must have been in Spanish.

"At first I thought maybe the marks signified other, smaller, islands not on any normal map, and I wondered what he was looking for.

"Then I thought maybe they were shipping routes or known fishing sweet spots. That was until we met Nicolas.

"I don't know about you, but he doesn't strike me as a fisherman. He's built like someone who spends a lot of time indoors pouring over maps, not hauling fish out of rough seas."

Billy was speaking quietly in case Nicolas was along the corridor in his room, or worse standing a few feet from their own room straining his ears.

"Yeh, he looks more bookish," agreed Jake, not wanting to add any further opinion in case he broke Billy's flow.

"I know, right? He could be an explorer of some sort, but I don't think so.

"He's positioned himself in this guest house, in the middle of the jungle, almost completely off the grid. I don't think because he's hiding his discoveries, I think he's hiding himself. He's scared.

37

"Last night I went downstairs to have a cigarette in the garden, where I'd first met him. I couldn't sleep and my head was buzzing with all these *theories*.

"I was quiet as I didn't want to wake any of you, and I definitely didn't want to wake him. But as soon as I got halfway across the living room, there he was, our man, Nicolas, outside on the decking.

"He had his back to me and was facing the jungle path. I froze when I saw him. I don't think he heard me or knew I was there. He didn't turn around at any rate.

"I stayed there, transfixed, watching him for what felt like hours, but it was probably no more than fifteen or twenty minutes.

"He smoked a cigarette, but other than that, nothing. He just stood there facing that horrible looking path."

Billy paused, gauging their reactions.

"But… why?" Issy asked.

"I think, he was on guard. I came back upstairs, careful not to make a sound, but I couldn't sleep. I've been going over everything all night.

"The maps. He's not a fisherman, and I don't think he's some kind of explorer either. He's afraid, and I think he's not alone.

"Those markings are *sightings*. Of what I don't know, but I'm not sure I want to find out. Whatever it is I think Nicolas is hiding from it—or *him*."

The final word hung in the air for far longer than any of them wanted, but no one knew what to say to break the silence.

They all knew who Billy was talking about. The sinister figure with long dark hair and a grey beard who'd tried to kill them.

He'd chased them across Barbados and they'd only just escaped.

"If you're right," Jake started, making everyone jump with the sound of his voice. "And he has followed us from Barbados, it can't just be him that Nicolas's scared of, surely? If he's got a room full of maps, and dozens of markings, they can't all be for just one man—"

"There must be more of them," Billy finished Jake's sentence.

Another silence fell over the room while the four of them thought about this new and highly unpleasant concept.

"What do you mean, more of them?" asked Issy.

"Maybe the man who chased us isn't alone. What if he's part of a group that goes around terrorising islanders? What if we were just in the wrong place at the wrong time before?" Billy said.

"He's tracking us," Amy said quietly, her eyes blackening. "It was no accident he found us."

Issy, Billy, and Jake looked at her surprised, and a little unnerved. No one wanted to question how she seemed so certain, and they kept their mouths shut.

"And there will be others," she said, standing up from Billy's bed. "We need to find the next clue, before they do."

"Amy's right. The more time we spend trying to find out what Nicolas was up to the more it'll distract us from our original course, the next anchor," Jake agreed, still unsettled by Amy's sudden change in mood, and appearance. Her eyes were darker than he'd ever seen them.

"Sure, but we're back to square one, how do we get to it?" Billy asked. "The symbol that looks like a compass led us to the first clue in Barbados, right? A sunken anchor inside a cave, well off the beaten path, pointing out to sea."

Jake nodded. "The same symbol is on this map." He held aloft the rum bottle with the Antigua map on its label.

"So, we have to assume if we can get there," he said, pointing at the compass symbol. "We are going to find another anchor, which hopefully will also be pointing out to sea like an arrow, and if we follow the line of wherever it's pointing, it will cross with the line from the first anchor, revealing where the third, hidden island is."

"But *how*?" Billy's frustration was boiling up again.

"It took us a few tries in Barbados, right? And the first anchor was really well hidden, which was probably why it was still undisturbed so many years later. We've just got to shoot in the general direction and hope we get lucky, like last time," Jake said, trying to stay calm.

Billy looked at him his mouth opening and closing like a fish. "He's right. I haven't got a better idea," he conceded eventually. "Ladies?"

Issy and Amy shrugged and shook their heads.

"Right, might as well make a start then. That path I saw going in to the jungle, shit-scary as it looks, is probably our best bet, right?" Billy said reluctantly.

"Let's go a little way along it and see if we can find a way to get up here," he said, pointing to the compass symbol on the map.

CHAPTER 9: LOST

The expedition had started well enough. The path leading in to the jungle appeared to be used fairly regularly, with most of the overhanging leaves and creepers cut back, allowing them to keep to a brisk but comfortable pace.

They'd agreed to keep their conversations to a minimum, and light. They'd said it was to reduce the risk of alerting anyone to their whereabouts, which was true, but more than that they wanted to push the horrors that seemed to be chasing them out of their minds.

Billy, in particular, had been keen to keep what he'd seen on their arrival locked down. He did not want to imagine more of those *things* writhing in the undergrowth, let alone contemplate out loud whether they would attack people.

Despite his best efforts he was, however, unable to stop himself thinking about what would happen if they accidentally stumbled into some sort of lizard nest, and, after an hour or so of walking at a steady pace, he was extremely relieved to see the path open out on to a small unspoiled bay.

The beach, with light pink sand and shallow water stretching far out to sea, was exquisite and made even more picturesque by the fringe of big coconut trees with huge green leaves framing the scene and offering shade.

"We need to get up high, but I can't see any obvious way. Short break then we carry on. Looks like the jungle path continues on the other side of the beach?" Jake said, setting his roll-top backpack down on the sand.

He reached inside and pulled out a large bottle of water before offering it around.

Issy took the bottle, her grey vest top dark at the edges with sweat. It was approaching midday and must have been at least thirty-five degrees Celsius (ninety-five degrees Fahrenheit).

She handed the bottle back to Jake, wiped the sweat from her eyes and forehead with the back of her hand and found a shady spot to rest. Jake flopped down next to her, his t-shirt soaked through too.

Billy stayed with Amy a few feet away while she rummaged through her yellow backpack looking for something. After a minute or two she pulled out four bananas and a pack of Oreos, and began handing them around the group.

Billy watched her, raised an eyebrow, and smiled as he took a banana and scooped out a melted chocolate biscuit.

"What?" Amy snapped.

"Nothing, I just didn't have you down for the mothering type, that's all." Billy laughed.

"Shut up," she replied, trying to keep a straight face but unable to stop her lips curling ever so slightly. She walked over to Issy and positioned herself cross-legged on the sand next to her friend.

Billy remained standing. "Ten minutes here then let's push on?" he said.

The others agreed without enthusiasm, feeling their bodies melt into the ground. The heat and humidity had sucked out their energy and the translucent shallow water ahead looked far more appealing than the thick rainforest to their right.

The sea couldn't have been more tranquil, but their memories off the shores of Barbados were still far too raw for them even to dip a toe. They'd experienced pure horror in deeper, darker waters, and even the thought of wading into the shallows filled them with dread.

"If we have time maybe we can come back here?" suggested Issy, lifting the big bottle of water to her lips once more and taking another warm mouthful of water.

She didn't get a response. Billy was engrossed in trying to get a phone signal, Amy was reapplying sun cream to her face, and to her left Jake was resting his eyes.

Issy studied his messy blond-brown hair. She watched as a bead of sweat ran through the blond stubble on his rounded chin, dripped onto his slender neck, and worked its way across his collarbone.

Her eye was drawn to the rope tattooed around his left wrist resting on his stomach, rising and falling in time with his breathing. The tattoo had fascinated her since they'd met. Her gaze then switched to his right arm, and the boat carefully inked on his forearm with the name *Adelaide* carved into the side.

She was following the lines of its perfectly crafted sails when Jake's eyes opened a fraction, then fully when he caught Issy staring.

She froze. *Busted.* Instinctively, she hurled the little warm liquid that remained in the bottle straight at Jake's face, the majority hitting his forehead.

In retaliation, he blew hard through his lips spraying her with water as she spun her head away.

"I would say get a room, but we are currently being hunted down by either a lone killer or vicious gang, or both, so probably best if we keep moving," Billy said, hauling Jake's backpack up on one shoulder ready to take his turn, before stretching out his arm and offering his hand to help Jake up.

Jake ignored the comment, gripped his friend's much larger hand, and let him pull him to his feet.

Issy got up too, exchanging a sheepish glance with Jake, then went over to take a turn with Amy's yellow backpack.

The four of them took a final look along their own private paradise beach, not lingering on the long stretch of shallow clear water for too long in case its whisper lured them in and off their course.

"Right. Let's go find that anchor," Billy said, assuming command once more.

When they'd been in Barbados Billy's size had often slowed him down and forced the others to wait. He'd felt a burden to the group on more than one occasion, and he was determined to make up for it.

He'd never been especially fit and had the makings of a beer belly already, despite only just turning twenty-six. But he was also one hundred eighty-eight centimetres (six feet two), his broad frame carried any extra weight well, and he was the strongest among them. He marched ahead picking up the jungle trail at the opposite edge of the beach to the side they'd entered, Jake followed behind, with Amy just about keeping up behind him, and Issy comfortably trotting along at the back, protectively keeping sight of her friend in front of her.

Issy had been worried about her ever since Amy had walked in on her fiancé with another woman around a month ago. Amy had been a mess and had begged Issy to come away with her on vacation. A couple of weeks away from everything that reminded her of her fiancé, some sun, sea, cocktails, and a few other distractions was what they'd had in mind.

Fearing Amy would totally come off the rails if she said no, Issy had made up a sob story and bagged some time away from work. She was contracted to one of the better London football teams and they'd been really understanding, making Issy feel even worse about the lie. She was in the middle of a break-through season, too, with one of the biggest clubs in France chasing her signature. It hadn't been ideal, but Amy was more important, and there hadn't been much of a choice.

Had she known their island escape would turn into such an ordeal she might have suggested a staycation and locked themselves in her Finsbury Park apartment for two weeks instead. But they were here now, and they'd already gone through too much to turn back.

She looked ahead at Amy's bare, smooth legs marching along in front of her, protruding from her blue tropical floral print shorts and matching top. She had black cat eye sunglasses on and was wearing her bright orange lipstick again.

Despite always looking like she belonged on a photoshoot more than an expedition, Amy had proven remarkably resilient, and unpredictable. Issy never knew which Amy she was going to get these days, but she was determined to look out for her, no matter what.

As they trudged along, the heat still seared even under the shade of the coconut trees, but the thick canopy blocked out most of the sunlight. The outstretched branches meant they had to be really careful when making their next steps.

They hiked single file, their progress slowing as the rainforest jungle thickened, barely exchanging a word between them.

No longer distracted by gentle waves and pink shores, and with no obvious space to run should they need to, their thoughts turned to their pursuer, or worse, pursuers plural. Imagining there could be more than one of *him* out there was not something any of them wanted to dwell on, but it was impossible not to think about it.

They'd first seen him after finding the first clue. They'd not long re-found civilisation, and had been celebrating their discovery, and survival, in a quiet restaurant they'd come across, when Issy had seen a man with a wide brim hat and long coat, loitering in the shadows at a distance across the road from them.

Shortly after that they'd experienced the horror of witnessing him up close too. He'd always worn his hat low, but they'd seen his long, dark grey hair and beard of the same colour, along with a glimpse of his dark eyes that none of them could erase from their memories, no matter how hard they tried.

Sharing each other's thoughts, they picked up the pace and strode more purposefully forward in to the undergrowth.

Another hour passed and frustration was growing.

"There's no up!" said Jake. Since they'd left the beach, every time they thought they'd found a path that would lead them to the cliffs on their right, it had been a dead end.

Amy stopped. "Let's take a break."

She dropped her bag to the ground and leaned back against one of the larger trees nearest to her, lifting one leg up off the ground and placing the sole of her foot flat against the trunk. She turned her head in the direction they'd been walking, scanning for a possible way up, or at this point, out.

She looked to Billy like she was posing for a magazine, and he couldn't help but look at the amount of thigh that was showing.

He was about to look away, realising he'd been staring too long, when something caught his eye on the floor among the creepers. His thick humid breath caught in his throat.

The same type of stripe-backed lizard that he'd witnessed massacre a turtle twice its size on their way in, was scuttling swiftly towards Amy's standing leg.

He could feel a scream scratching at his lungs, but nothing came out.

He just watched, paralysed, as the creature flew across the mud and vines, its beady-eyes set, its arms and legs a blur, and its teeth bared.

Then something surreal happened.

The lizard skidded to a halt a few feet from Amy's standing leg, scattering twigs and leaves in its wake. Its expression, and body-language, changed suddenly, as though it had hit an electric fence.

For a second it rose to its hind legs, looking defensive, deciding whether to fight, or flee back in to the jungle as far away as possible.

It sucked at the air through its sharp teeth and Billy, gripped, saw a tiny tongue dart in and out of its mouth, repulsing him.

Then it flipped its entire body over to face the direction it had come charging out from, and it ran, its tail sweeping side to side, tripping over the odd hidden branch in its hurry to get away, spraying more dirt and leaves behind it.

"What the..." Billy stammered, sweaty, and shaking.

Jake had been spraying Issy with insect repellent and the pair of them had been oblivious. Hearing Billy's stuttering voice they turned to see what was going on, hurrying over to help him as soon as they saw the panic in his eyes.

Amy reached up to her face, took her sunglasses between thumb and forefinger and placed them up above her forehead so that they were resting on her hair, and she could get a better look at what was going on.

Her dark eyes were again bigger than they usually were, and she was examining Billy.

Issy and Jake put their arms around a big shoulder each and guided him to sit on the ground, but he refused to budge and panicked more whenever they tried.

"Breathe, breathe, that's it. What happened?" Issy asked, when he was a touch calmer.

Billy opened his mouth to tell them, but then he stopped, catching Amy's eye. One of her eyebrows was ever so slightly raised. He wasn't sure, and didn't want to believe it, but he felt like she was conveying a silent threat to him.

He took another moment.

"I'm okay, honestly, thank you," he said, gently pushing them away.

"I just saw one of those things again," he began, then realised only Jake knew what he was talking about.

He looked again at Amy. She hadn't moved a muscle, her eyes still locked on him.

"What *things?*" asked Issy, sounding panicky herself.

Billy retold the story he'd told Jake, not being too graphic to totally scare Issy—he now realised he needn't have worried about Amy on that score—but graphic enough to justify his recent reaction.

47

"Yeh, I just saw it run past, over there. It was bigger than the one I saw on the beach and it... it just really freaked me out," he ended weakly, but certain he'd made the right call in not telling the whole story. He'd talk to Jake later, in private.

Amy looked satisfied. She removed her glasses from on top of her head and placed them back on her face, picked up her backpack, and stood waiting for the others to gather themselves together.

"Let's keep moving," she instructed, turning away from the rest of the group and striding off in to the jungle.

Issy and Jake exchanged looks and shrugged. Issy chased off after Amy and Jake made sure Billy was okay, the pair of them following behind at a slightly slower pace.

"What happened, really?" Jake hissed, when a bit of a gap had opened up between them.

"I..." Billy began then looked up ahead. The gap wasn't big enough for his liking, "I'll tell you later, when we're back in our room," he whispered at a level he hoped Jake could still hear, but no one else.

Jake nodded and they upped the pace.

After another gruelling hour in the heat they'd made no further progress, and they still had the return journey to make. The few supplies they'd brought with them had long gone and tempers were frayed to breaking point.

Jake and Billy had quarrelled over a forked trail they'd found half an hour back and now both were snapping at each other sarcastically.

Issy had been trying to keep the peace but even her eternally optimistic outlook had been tested beyond its limit, and now she couldn't care less if the two of them were arguing, she just wanted to get out of the sweaty, suppressing jungle and into a swimming pool.

But it was Amy's mood that had darkened most of all.

She'd barely said a word for the last hour, and had stuck to the front, driving them forward. The only time she'd fallen back was when she thought they'd found a breakthrough, only for each hopeful shout to turn into another false dawn, darkening Amy's mood even further.

"I told you we should have spent more time on mapping out the area, a day wasted—"

"A day wasted... what?" interrupted Billy. "Chill the fuck out. This anchor has been buried for three hundred years, just like the last one was. No one found it in all that time, what difference does one day make?"

"It makes a difference because we're most likely being hunted! And whoever is hunting us is probably after the same thing, so it—"

Issy screamed as loudly as she could.

Billy and Jake stopped bickering and fell silent. Amy snapped her head around sharply and sent a look like thunder through all of them before scanning the trees around them carefully.

"Stop it, okay? Just stop. We've got to get out of here, I'm done. We're done," Issy said, shaking. "For today, I mean," she added quickly.

"Sorry, you're right, we're fucked. We hoped we'd get lucky today, but we didn't have a contingency plan in place if we didn't. Let's go back and regroup," Jake said, feeling defeated and stupid.

He looked at Billy to see if they were still fighting and saw his friend felt as bad as he did. He looked a state too. His forehead was dripping with sweat and his sleeveless light blue and white striped shirt was stuck unflatteringly to his chest and back.

"We're cool," he said to Jake reading his thoughts. "You don't look so hot yourself." He smiled, giving a small nod in the direction of Jake's soaking wet top.

"We've got a last sip of water left, I think. Let's finish that then find our way back to the guest house," Jake said, moving to fetch his backpack back off Billy's shoulder.

Amy had quietly made her way back into the middle of the group.

"No," she hissed.

She was different again, and no one wanted to argue. After an awkward silence, Issy moved a tentative step closer to her friend. "Come on, Ames. We can come back tomorrow, once we've got a bit more of a plan," she said.

Amy did not look happy, nor did she look herself, but the Amy in front of them eventually nodded, sensing there was no way she could win this argument.

"Sure," she managed, cracking her orange lips just enough to let the words out before resetting her stony expression.

The journey home was relatively uneventful, and on the whole, quiet. No one had energy for anything other than survival.

Amy had dropped to the back and even Issy was too tired to follow behind her and make sure she was okay, and not a danger to herself or, as they were beginning to realise was more likely, others.

At one point as they were crossing the idyllic stretch of beach Amy had, to Issy, Jake, and Billy's utter dismay, stopped and frozen as still as a statue halfway along the sand, her eyes glued to a single location deep within the coconut trees.

Issy had dropped back to see what was going on, but she couldn't see anything, and Amy wouldn't talk about it.

The others could only assume she'd either seen someone, something, perhaps one of those creepy striped lizards, or it was her mind doing strange things to her, which seemed to be happening more frequently with every passing hour.

Too tired to entertain the first two options they pushed the unpleasant thoughts to the back of their minds, where they were building quite a collection, and opted to go with the third explanation—that Amy had temporarily lost her mind.

Worried Amy would drop to the ground and refuse to move at any moment, each of them breathed a sigh of relief when she started walking again. Issy locked her arm through her friend's, marched her back to Billy and Jake, and they walked more or less as a foursome for the remainder of the journey.

When they finally recognised the path that led to the back of their guest house Jake, Billy, and Issy were practically euphoric.

"I never thought I'd be so happy to see this creepy little place," Jake said, finding a final burst of energy now he knew they were almost there.

The only person not smiling, was Amy, who's dark eyes were trained on a ledge high above them to her left.

CHAPTER 10: SECRETS

"What really happened out there?" Jake asked when they were safely back in their own room.

Billy sat bare-chested in his black chino shorts on his bed. He'd discarded his soaking wet shirt as soon as he'd come through the door and it lay in a soggy, crumpled heap on the floor.

Jake noted the large gash still clearly visible on the side of Billy's stomach from their exploits on the last island and took some comfort to see the wound didn't look too angry and appeared to be healing nicely.

There was no aircon in the room, but they did have an ancient-looking ceiling fan that was on and whirring as fast as its one setting allowed, and a small window which opened out straight in to the jungle, offering a very close-up view of the trees and little-to-no-breeze.

"I saw one of those things again, why is it just me that keeps seeing those things? They're disgusting. Anyway, I saw one and it was tearing towards Amy's leg. I wanted to scream, I mean I wanted to yell, but I felt like I was going to scream... and then I just froze." Billy said the last part more quietly, unhappy about his inaction, and doubly ashamed because he'd already been trying to make up for his perceived weakness on the last expedition.

"We've seen some weird things since we've been on this trip mate," Jake said, wanting to reassure his friend but unable to find the right words.

"It was haring towards her leg and I could already see it ripping into her like it did that turtle, but then... it just stopped, it looked absolutely terrified. It was like a loud gun had gone off in its head telling it that unless it got the hell out of there it was going to die, horribly.

"Then it turned and ran, I mean fast, much faster than when it had been on the front foot.

"That thing was petrified, I've never seen fear like that in a fucking animal!" Billy said, frustrating himself with his words and how ridiculous they must have sounded.

There was silence while Jake processed what he was being told.

"Scared of what?" he asked.

Billy looked at him, and Jake could see he was afraid too.

"Amy," he said quietly.

Jake shuddered. He wasn't entirely surprised and didn't doubt his friend's account of events for a second.

"She's not herself," Jake said. "We need to keep a closer eye on her, it's happening more and more."

Billy nodded. They didn't discuss *it* in any more detail, they both knew what the other was talking about.

The episodes had happened often enough now that they could even spot the signs before they happened.

She would normally go quiet or stop talking altogether, and if she did say something it was always serious, and always to do with finding the anchor.

But her biggest tell was her eyes. Her pupils swelled to an unnatural size and her eyes filled with darkness. Both Billy and Jake struggled to maintain eye contact when her eyes had *turned*. They also suspected that Amy, or a version of Amy, knew that her eyes gave her away. She'd started wearing her sunglasses all the time, rarely taking them off even when they were indoors.

Billy nodded again. "Yeh, we'll keep a closer eye on her," he repeated.

"Keeping an eye on her isn't really the problem though," Billy whispered, unsatisfied with their solution after letting Jake's words digest. "The problem is what we're going to *do* about it if we notice she's switched again."

It was Jake's turn to nod. He'd been on the receiving end of those eyes, and he'd withered just as Billy had done. He certainly didn't fancy confronting her when she was in that state.

Jake sat, thinking.

"Okay, so we try and keep her as Amy as much as we can," he declared.

Billy furrowed his brow but didn't interrupt.

"She seems to switch more often when we're focussed on finding the anchor, or when we're in danger. I mean the two things also kind of go hand in hand."

"Agreed," Billy said.

"So, tomorrow, let's break it up a bit. Let's take a day off, lay low somewhere and just try and get her back on side, back to how she was, *is*, you know what I mean," Jake said.

Billy slowly nodded his head. "I do. It's a good idea, the only problem is—we are here to find that anchor. Without it we can't find the third island, and if we can't find that we can't find the treasure, assuming there is a treasure.

"How are we supposed to do all that without, I don't know, stressing her out and making her all fucking demonic again?" Billy asked half rhetorically.

Another silence.

"Guess it's the best we've got," Jake said finally.

CHAPTER 11: THE BEACH

"Come on, Ames, it'll be fun," Issy said brightly, pulling her friend along the little path by her hand.

Breakfast had been a real battle of wills. Amy, unsurprising to Billy and Jake, had adamantly rejected their suggestion of a day at the beach, and refused point blank to sit around on the little bay they'd found the day before, 'Giving our enemies a head start,' as she'd put it.

But they'd anticipated her reaction, and their tactic was to weigh heavy on Issy, who was the only one who still held any sway over Amy when she was less than her usual self.

"Get Issy set on this, and I reckon Amy will fall in line," Jake had said optimistically when they'd been planning what they'd say in their room the night before.

"And what if she doesn't?" Billy had asked.

"Fuck knows, mate," Jake laughed. "Got any better ideas?"

Billy hadn't any better ideas. "Issy it is then."

They'd caught some luck when Issy had appeared for breakfast ahead of Amy, who was just finishing getting ready.

It had given them an opportunity to reveal their plan, replacing the parts about stopping Amy's personality from splitting with. "We just think she could do with a break."

Issy knew instantly what they were getting at and had been racking her brain to come up with something to help too. She'd hardly slept for worry, and longed for things to go back to how they were.

Issy had been working for a design company near Kings Cross when they'd first met, and she'd been given the task of showing Amy around. Even on her first day she was the most confident person in the room.

Over lunch Issy had discovered how Amy had met her fiancé in a bar in Sydney. She'd just got a job at a media agency and had been out with her new colleagues at the end of her first week around Darling Harbour. She'd hit it off with a British guy named Tony and, when her new acquaintances left, she'd snuck him into the women's toilets, before going back to his place in Manly. A few weeks later he dropped the bombshell that he needed to go home, that he had a big job offer waiting for him in England, but he wanted her to come with him. He'd then gotten down on one knee and proposed—and she had said yes.

Issy remembered how excited Amy had been retelling the story to her, and how Issy had tried to push down her own cynicism; the first thought having come to mind was that they'd never last. She'd been right, ultimately, but she still loved Amy's lust for life and badly wanted her back to the way she was.

When Billy and Jake suggested a day at the beach so they could regain their strength and their spirit, especially Amy, she was immediately on board.

And, as Jake had hoped, with her weighing in, the three of them had won the battle of wills at breakfast, and found themselves in their beachwear, with towels and a few beers, heading down the rainforest path to the tranquil beach, instead of another day of jungle trekking. And even Amy, the Amy they were friends with, was extremely glad about that.

"Heads up!" Billy yelled hurling the green and pink tennis ball he'd found in the guest house high in the air above Amy and Issy up ahead of them.

Issy turned, caught the flight of the ball against the bright blue sky and jogged backwards to position herself underneath it, splashing into the shallows to align herself with the ball's trajectory.

She plucked it out of the air with one hand, swung her arm back in the same motion and launched the ball high in the air back towards Billy.

"Nice!" she heard Jake's voice from back up the beach.

It was then she realised where she was standing. Fear rose from the balls of her feet shooting up through her entire body, leaving her breathless and rooted to the spot.

"*Stay calm, stay calm, stay calm,*" she repeated unable to stop her panic escalating.

It was the first time any of them had gone near the water since Barbados.

The waterline was barely up to her knees, and she could see every detail of the sea bed; besides the odd shell, and a few pieces of sea weed gently floating on the waves there was nothing. But it didn't stop her thinking about that night, and what could have been.

That had been the first time Amy had gone completely off key, after they'd opened, and finished, one of the rum bottles. It had made all of them feel funny, but it had affected Amy in a much deeper and more disturbing way.

After that all hell had broken loose. Amy had stolen the maps, then a boat, and had made an unexplainable dash for the first clue, all on her own.

The others had chased after her, stealing jet skis in order to do so. At first Billy and Jake had been full of anger, but Issy had known her friend was no thief, and had been worried sick.

She was right to have been. Amy hadn't made it to the first clue— something had found her first.

Issy had always been level-headed and hard to scare with myths and ghost stories, and she'd never believed in monsters, even as a small child.

Until this trip.

What had found Amy and her boat had nearly killed her, and when Issy and the others caught up and found her, it turned on them too.

She had a flashback of fins, and teeth, and black eyes writhing in wild frothing waters.

Breathing fast, she hurriedly searched the shallow water around her, checking for the slightest ripple that looked out of place.

As fast as she could, while simultaneously trying to disturb the water as little as possible, she waded back the four or five steps to the sand, where Jake was waiting for her.

"It's okay. Come here," he said, taking her shaking arms and guiding them around him as he moved in closer to give her a hug.

Jake had seen her freeze in the water and known immediately why. He'd told Billy to stay with Amy and had gone straight away to fish her out.

"There's nothing here," he said trying to reassure her, unconvinced by his own words. He scanned the water over her shoulder and was hugely relieved to see nothing but waves.

"I'm still not going back in." She laughed, her colour gradually returning.

"That's fair. How about a walk along the sea front?" Jake asked.

Issy looked back up the beach to make sure Amy was okay, then fell in step with Jake along the water's edge.

He thought about taking her hand, and half-reached out only to change his mind. Issy noticed his awkward jerky movement, and for a moment neither of them knew what to say.

They'd flirted before, but before anything more could develop horror had interrupted lust and they'd been forced to focus on survival. Any feelings they'd had for each other had been put on ice, and they still had plenty of steps to make up before they got anywhere near hand holding.

"I never asked you before," said Issy, picking up her train of thought from the beach the day before. "What's the story behind your tattoos? What's this one?" she asked, pointing to the rope on his left arm. "And who's Adelaide?" she asked, switching her finger to the boat stretching up his inner right forearm.

"It's… I don't know. I got them just after I turned eighteen." He paused, as if weighing up what to tell her. "I just wanted to look cool, I guess."

"Ah, rubbish! Come on. They've got a meaning, I know it. Tell me." Issy laughed, pushing his shoulder and knocking him off balance.

He looked at her and grinned helplessly. It felt good to be doing something other than searching, running, or hiding.

"Go on, if you tell me you get to ask me one question, and I *have* to tell you the answer, truthfully." She smiled, biting on the end of her tongue.

His mind went in to meltdown. There were plenty of questions he wanted to ask but all of them made him cringe when he role-played them in his mind, and the thought of asking them to Issy's face, out loud, just made him go red.

Then he thought of something.

"Okay, deal," he said confidently, holding out his hand ready to shake on it.

"Hang on. What have you thought of? Maybe I didn't think this through." Issy laughed.

"Too late. This rope is a sailor's knot, look it has no start or finish, and represents eternity. Dad told me it was to remind sailors of loved ones waiting for them while they were at sea, and the strength of their love, stuff like that," he said, getting embarrassed.

"Uh huh, so who's waiting for you? Adelaide?" Issy asked, tracing her finger along the rope around Jake's wrist.

"Adelaide's the name of my dad's boat, and it was the name of his dad's boat, and the name of his dad's boat, and so on. Dad said he doesn't know where it started but it's been a family tradition for years," Jake explained.

"That's really cool," Issy said, and she meant it. She wanted to say more but couldn't think of anything. Then her eyes lit up.

"Don't forget your question," Issy prompted coquettishly, remembering their deal. "You're a bloke, so I'm guessing your mind went straight to the gutter. Come on then, let's hear it. What do you want to know?"

Jake was desperate to ask her about Amy, about whether Issy knew what was happening to her, and whether she still trusted her.

Now they had a moment alone he also really wanted to ask her what she thought, about the whole thing. Were they right to keep chasing some imaginary treasure even though it had already nearly killed them, more than once—but more than that, he wanted to know if she really *believed* it existed, and did she really think they could find it? And if they did, what would she do with all the money?

He'd spent years daydreaming about what he'd do if he suddenly had limitless means, and to him, this was his one shot.

He'd grown up in Falmouth, a small town in Cornwall, with a rich sailing history and the world's third largest natural deep-water harbour. His parents owned and ran a little café, and his dad also took tourists out on his boat to top up their income. They'd never had a lot of cash growing up, and it hadn't bothered Jake in the slightest. But as he'd gotten a bit older he'd started to notice how much money could affect people.

His dad's brother, Tim, had suddenly come into a small fortune when Jake was in his early teens, when a big construction company wanted to buy the land his house was built on. Tim didn't have to think about it for long, cashed in, and moved to a much bigger house in a posh village, regularly inviting Jake's parents over, mainly so he could show off. Jake remembered his dad's face as he listened politely to Tim lecturing him about bathroom wall tiles, and how you should only buy the expensive ones otherwise you might as well not have a bathroom at all. Jake didn't think his father was jealous, in fact he knew he wasn't. He preferred his life to Tim's tenfold, but he could tell he *hated* being made to feel small.

Jake swore when he was older he'd have money of his own, decent money. Not so he could laud it over people like Tim had done, but so that his dad never had to feel small ever again. Not that his dad wanted fancy tiles, he was more a, 'It does the job' kind of man. But there were things he did want, like a new boat, and to take his mum on more trips abroad. All their money had gone on Jake and their family business. They were happy, Jake knew that, but he wanted them to be able to enjoy a few more luxuries, they deserved it.

He'd wanted to travel, too, to see as much of the world as he could but, until this trip, he'd hardly been anywhere. He'd just *thought* about the places he would go to, if he ever had the chance. Jake even had a bucket list of countries, prioritised in the order he most wanted to go to them—the Caribbean as a whole had been right at the top. Pirate stories had been told to him for as long as he could remember, and the idea of adventuring off to wild tropical islands had always captured his imagination.

He wanted badly to tell Issy all about his past, and his ideas, and he realised in that moment he wanted her to be a part of them almost as much. But he resisted the urge, knowing if he blurted out all of that the mood would turn serious, he'd miss his chance, and he guessed she'd probably run a mile.

Right now, he had an opportunity to edge further away from the 'friend zone' that he was worried he was already one foot in, and he knew if he didn't take it he'd regret it later on.

He looked at her unbelievably toned body in her red bikini, told himself to shut the hell up and stop overthinking everything and just ask the hot girl something dirty.

"Best place you've ever done it?" he asked, eventually, feeling his face burn up as soon as the words had escaped his mouth.

"Ha! I knew it! You're all the same," she said.

"Well?" he said, attempting a smile, and accepting it was too late to back out now.

"Bonnet of my ex's Volkswagen Golf. He was supposed to be giving me a lift to training, but the mood took us, we found somewhere quiet-ish and we just kind of went at it," she said, grinning.

Jake's mouth fell open slightly, but he couldn't think of what to say next. Issy burst into laughter.

"Come on," she said. "Let's go and check on the other two."

CHAPTER 12: HORIZON

Jake was about to follow Issy back up the beach when he saw something.

"Wait!" he said.

Issy spun around in the sand and saw Jake pointing out to sea.

"Is that a… ship?" she asked.

"I think so, but it keeps *fading*. It's like it's shrouded in mist. Wait, look, it's clearer now," Jake said.

The vessel was big, but quite far away. Jake and Issy inspected it carefully as it sat unmoving on the horizon directly in front of where they were standing, before it disappeared again.

"It's a warship," said Jake quietly.

"What?"

"A warship. It's a frigate, full-rigged, and I'd guess it's about twelve hundred centimetres (forty feet) long, but it's at a bit of an angle so it's hard to tell.

"They used to have around forty cannons on them, or more, but this has got to be a replica. It must be for tourists, look it's even got a black flag, I can't quite make out the symbols on it though," Jake said, pointing.

"What does that mean?" Issy asked, confused.

"Pirates, a black flag meant the crew on board the ship were pirates.

"They didn't always have the biggest ships, or the most men, but they were feared for being the most ruthless. Raising the black flag was to let other ships know they were pirates and it would be better for them if they just surrendered," Jake said.

He caught Issy's raised eyebrow.

"I'm from Falmouth, I live in Bristol, and work in a pub that pirates used to drink in." He shrugged. "And my dad's really into all that stuff too. He used to tell me all the old sailor stories when I was a kid."

As they stared at the ship, it faded out of view again.

"How is that possible?" Issy asked, squinting her eyes as though it would help solidify the warship.

"That, I don't know," said Jake. "That ship gives me the creeps."

"If it is for tourists rather them than me," Issy agreed.

"You don't think… it's connected? It can't be *him*, right?" Jake asked, picturing the sinister figure with the black coat and grey beard standing on the deck, looking right back at them. He shuddered.

"We've seen some pretty weird stuff but a fading pirate ship's taking it a bit far. It's got to be a tourist thing, and it's just some unusual weather, localised mist maybe?" Issy said, almost hopefully.

"Yeh, you're right," Jake said, still unsettled by what he'd seen, and unconvinced localised mist was even a real thing.

"Should we mention it to the others?" he added.

Issy didn't answer straight away. She looked for the ship, which had faded so much now it was difficult to find again.

Telling Billy would be no big deal, but she knew that's not what Jake was asking.

If she told her friend she had no idea how she was going to react, but on the other hand she was too afraid not to.

"Yeh, we should tell her," Issy replied. She knew Jake was worried about Amy; she was too. She was becoming more unpredictable by the day.

If things carried on the way they were they'd have to say or do something about it, not that she had any idea what. But she did know that to have any chance of standing up to her when she was—*not herself*—it would take all three of them. And even then she didn't feel confident it would make any difference.

The ship had faded so much it had become part sea and part cloud. No one would notice even if they were looking directly at it, but Jake and Issy knew it was still there.

"Come on. Let's go," Issy said, turning back up the beach again.

Jake followed, grateful for the few moments he'd had with Issy before something else had happened.

He didn't know what the ship was, but somehow he just *knew* it had nothing to do with tourists. Whoever, or whatever, was on that ship had wanted to hurt them. He'd felt it.

As they got closer they heard Amy laughing, her own laugh, and then saw Billy's chest covered in most of a bottle of sun cream.

"Everything okay?" Jake said cautiously as he approached the two of them.

Billy was grinning and Amy was laughing so much she'd gone red and had tears running down her cheeks. She snorted involuntarily trying to gather in air and managed to pull herself together a bit.

"What have you been up to, Pretty Boy?" Amy asked. She hadn't called Jake that for a while. It had been her way of teasing him for looking too clean cut when they'd first met, but it had turned into a term of endearment.

Jake smiled, he was just pleased to see that her sunglasses were by her side and her eyes were her own.

Issy and Jake found their beach towels and took their places next to each other.

"How can we tell her now?" Jake hissed in Issy's ear, trying to be as subtle as he could and hoping Amy would just assume they were flirting.

"She's back to normal, this'll just send her flying off the edge again," he said.

"We have to. If she finds out we kept something from her, I don't know what she'll do, but we should tell her.

"Also, I'm kind of scared, Jake. That didn't look like a tourist boat to me and it felt… I don't know it felt *something* and it shouldn't have felt anything," Issy added, panicking.

"What are you two talking about? Sounds heated," Amy chipped in. She'd been following their exchange and was resting on her elbows.

Billy sat up, wanting to hear too.

"We saw something on the water," said Jake, pushing himself up onto his knees and facing all three of them.

"It was a ship, but it looked, weird… It looked old, like seventeenth century old. We thought maybe it's for tourists but, it was only there for a minute or two and, it kept, *fading*."

Billy looked towards the sea trying to find what they were talking about.

"It's still there," Issy said, pointing. "It's really hard to make out now and kind of blends in with the clouds, but it's definitely there."

Billy couldn't see anything, but he could tell by their expressions this was no joke.

"What do you think it is?" he asked.

Before Jake or Issy had time to answer, Amy stood up and wrapped her palm print mini sarong over the top of her black bikini bottoms and started gathering their things together.

"They know we're here," she said flatly.

Jake, Issy, and Billy exchanged anxious, puzzled looks with each other.

66

"Move!" Amy ordered, bending down and picking up Billy's Giants t-shirt and throwing it at him.

They quickly grabbed their clothes and stuffed whatever they couldn't wear into one of the two bags before hurrying back to the jungle path, still only half dressed, making their way as quickly as they could towards the guest house.

Only Amy seemed to know what they were running from, but Billy, Jake, and Issy could guess, and that was enough to keep them moving.

There would be time for questions and details later if they could just make it to the sanctuary of their lodgings—although how safe the guest house really was none of them knew.

CHAPTER 13: STAND OFF

High up on a rocky ledge the Watchman packed away his spyglass and prepared to move.

He'd barely taken his eyes off Billy, Amy, Jake, and Issy since the night they'd arrived in Antigua, and the pressure to strike had been building with every passing hour since—but something had told him to hold back.

Wait.

He could have attacked the day before when they'd been lost in thick undergrowth, but their movements had been unpredictable. The odds had certainly been in his favour, but he needed to make *sure*. If he only got one shot, and he missed, the consequences would be grim.

The Watchman chose not to dwell on what awaited him if he failed, and instead focussed his mind on the task at hand.

He'd watched the blonde-haired woman and one of the men at the water's edge and he'd seen them freeze, feeling the same fear they'd felt at the sight of the ship on the horizon.

They're not supposed to be so close.

He'd seen Issy and Jake's reaction, and how quickly the four of them had packed up their things and fled after they'd told Amy and Billy—and he knew where they'd go next. He wouldn't get a better opportunity. He stood and looked out to sea in the direction of his ship.

It's time. Soon, it will be done.

He moved swiftly back to the hidden trail that had taken him to his vantage point, and began his descent, setting off at a fast pace knowing he only had a small window to close in on his target.

Despite his rapid movement he hardly made a sound, gliding across the wet mud and skilfully avoiding tree roots and stray branches.

The Watchman had calculated the ground he'd need to cover before their paths converged, and he needed to time it so that he could descend on them from the hidden trail at just the right moment.

He couldn't afford any mistakes, this was the most important kill he'd been tasked with in his life, and he'd used all his years of experience to make sure none of them had any chance of escaping from the trap he was springing.

His long hair sprayed out behind him as he pushed on, driving his legs forward, planting the thick soles of his black boots firmly on the more even ground, and avoiding the rocks and bumps, barely thinking about his next step. The trail was more than familiar to him, every bend and stump ingrained in his memory

Then he heard them. Not far up ahead.

The chatter had been faint and short, but he was certain it was them, which meant he was getting close.

He'd timed his attack perfectly, and his decision to wait an extra day was justified.

In a few more strides the same hidden trail Amy, Billy, Issy, and Jake were searching for would spit the Watchman out right above them. With the cover of the trees gone, the Watchman would be exposed, and if any of them looked up it would be impossible for them to miss him.

No matter now.

As the trail opened out, the Watchman slowed to see them just below, the dark-haired woman was at the front, then a small gap and the bigger man—the Watchman decided he would need to cut him down quickly to stamp out any possible retaliation before it happened—then the blonde woman, then the shorter man with the light hair at the back.

They were walking briskly, but at a pace far slower than his. He adjusted his footfall to stride in parallel with theirs, and prepared to strike, reaching inside his long coat for his double-edged dagger attached to his leather belt next to his hunting knife.

Arm raised to his chest he held his nerve a few more steps, waiting for the trail to turn sharply right. The bend was the exact spot he'd pinpointed to launch his attack, from there he could be upon them before any of them knew what was even happening.

He took a breath to steady himself, as he did before every battle, and was set to pounce when the woman with the dark hair snapped her head to her left and stared sharply up at him.

Stunned she'd known he was there, the Watchman almost stumbled off his perch in shock, catching his balance at the last moment. He froze, unsure for the first time in an ambush he'd instigated, of what to do next.

Amy kept walking but didn't take her eyes off him, her pupils black and swollen.

It can't be…

He felt dizzy. He kept his eyes on hers, more to make sure she didn't attack him than anything else.

Amy's lips curled into a nasty smile.

He knew then he was defeated and would have to face Captain Sands with empty hands. Despite the daunting prospect of facing the captain having failed, he still couldn't help but feel relieved as he slunk back into the rainforest.

If he'd really seen who he thought he'd seen in those unnatural eyes, he didn't have any option, he just needed to run.

Amy turned away satisfied and continued on her way to the guest house, the others in tow, oblivious that the man they feared the most had just fled in terror from the woman guiding them.

CHAPTER 14: STORM

On the way back Issy had been looking all around her as much as she could without causing herself to lose balance and fall over.

She was satisfied by what she'd found—absolutely nothing.

No murderous psychopath in a long dark coat, no island gang, and no deranged wildlife threatening to tear them apart. And they were almost back.

Then she felt the first massive drops of rain.

"Perfect." She sighed, trying to work out how far they had left to go.

She estimated they were only another ten minutes or so from the guest house, but the rain was now hammering down and they were getting soaked.

It reminded her of the one and only time her two older brothers, Harry and Joe, had taken her camping in Wales, and it had been a complete washout. Issy had secretly been happy about the rain as she rarely got to see them, and when she did it was never together at the same time. She thought they'd be able to stay inside, play cards, and just talk like they used to. She really missed that after they left home. Harry had joined the Air Force, and Joe had just gotten into trouble, falling in with a gang and even ending up in prison.

They'd camped on a cliff-top overlooking a bay. The weather had been so bad it had blown the tent down more than once and in the end they'd given up, deciding instead to march for the nearest pub, carrying bits of the tent between them.

It had taken them over an hour to find somewhere and they were soaked through. They'd taken it in turns to go to the bathrooms, taking with them the driest of their clothes from their backpacks, and standing underneath the hand dryer to warm themselves up.

Issy had tried to match them drink for drink, competitive as always, keeping up right until the pub neared closing, when she had to run from the table to be sick. At the time she'd been furious at herself, not for drinking too much, but for letting them win. But when she returned to the table to find Harry and Joe laughing and joking around like they used to, it suddenly didn't seem as important.

She wished they were with her so she could ask them what she should do about Amy, the trail, the people chasing them—all of it.

A deafening clap of thunder broke overhead followed by lightning tearing across the sky shortly after.

If we can just make it back. She pictured the guest house. It was creepy as hell but it was a lot less unsettling than being out in the open.

Strangely, she'd felt safe there. Despite being awake most of the night worrying about Amy, she'd felt like nothing could get them.

Whether that was true, she wasn't sure. She just knew that she'd rather be bolted up indoors than wading through mud that was turning rapidly into a river, completely vulnerable to whatever else was outside with them.

As the heavy rain fell the muddy torrent beneath them swelled, and their going slowed almost to a standstill, with the risk of losing a shoe increasing with each footstep.

"Yeh, this is going to take more than ten minutes," Issy grumbled, pulling her trailing leg carefully out of a particularly deep muddy puddle.

Amy was the only one who was still making significant headway.

Billy, who was watching behind her, marvelled at how she'd barely slowed down despite the atrocious conditions.

He assumed her weight, or lack of, was helping. She was the lightest among them and her wedge sandals seemed to almost glide on top of the sludge.

Finally, they made it back to the small slope leading up to the decking at the rear of the guest house; the steps that had been carved into the side of the tiny hill already washing away. Amy spotted the hazard and took control to shepherd the group up the final obstacle.

Billy climbed up easily in just a few big strides, turning as soon as he reached the top to catch Jake just in time before he could slide back down. Issy slipped a couple of times but clawed her way close enough for Billy and Jake to grab hold of an arm each, so they could haul her up the rest of the way.

Safely up, they called down to Amy who was still standing at the bottom. She took a final look into the dark, sodden jungle to make sure they weren't still being followed, before she marched up the slope without faltering once.

She pushed past the others, threw the patio door open, and walked over to a large map of the island, water dripping from her body and forming a pool where she stood.

She completely ignored Nicolas, who had screamed at her sudden entrance, and was trying to pull himself together.

He'd been lost in his maps and markings and hadn't heard anyone approach above the sound of the storm. Then the door had violently blown open, wind, and rain had charged in to the room, thunder and lightning ripping across the sky in the background, and at the centre of it all, was a wild looking woman in a black bikini, her dark hair, and tiny sarong with palm leaves on it—the only other of item of clothing she had on—flapping and swirling all around her.

Her alluring appearance stopped his fear long enough to take a proper look at his intruder, but as soon as he caught a glimpse of her hostile expression, and those dark eyes so full of fury, he swallowed hard and wished, more than anything, he'd stayed in his room to study his maps.

When the door had first flown open, just for an instant, he'd thought *they'd* finally come, but now, looking at the soaking wet demonic-looking young woman in front of him, he realised he would have preferred if they had.

73

As he finally registered that she was a guest in his guest house, mustering just enough courage to attempt to speak, Billy, Jake, and Issy piled through the still open doorway. They were even wetter than Amy and had sodden clumps of the rainforest floor clinging to their feet and ankles, as though it was as desperate as they were to escape whatever was out there.

"*Nicolas?*" Billy said, surprised to see him sitting shell-shocked in the corner. "You okay?"

Nicolas's words caught in his throat. He put down the maps he realised he was still gripping hold of as carefully as he could with his shaking hands. Then he tried again.

"Close the door," he said. "Now!"

Billy, Issy, and Jake's arrival had reassured him somewhat, but he still wasn't happy about Amy, who was waiting for them to shut the door and looked like she was ready to conduct a meeting.

Jake slid the door as far as it would go until he heard it click into place.

"And lock it," Nicolas said, monitoring Jake's work unhappily.

Jake did as he was told and sat with the others on the L-shaped sofa. Nicolas stayed in his corner chair and Amy stood facing all of them.

"We gave them a day, and they found us. We should have looked for the trail again yesterday," Amy declared, pacing left and right as she spoke.

Issy, Billy, and Jake wondered how she *knew* they'd found them, and how she *knew* who *they* were, but they could see she was in no mood for questions and kept quiet.

But Nicolas had a fair idea.

"The trail that goes up to the cliffs?" he asked.

Amy scrutinised him carefully, making him flinch.

"Yes," she said. "That's the good news." Her lips curled into an unnerving smile. "Thanks to *them*, we now know where it is."

Jake, Billy, and Issy shot each other looks of utter confusion then stared at Amy eager to know more.

Nicolas sank back slightly in his chair, his usefulness to the group vanishing as quickly as it had appeared, and Amy's smile frightening him even more than when she'd first come in.

"The beginning of the trail is not far in to the jungle and runs parallel to the beach path. I saw one of them on it," she said.

"*He's here!*" Issy panicked.

Issy, Jake, and Billy looked to Amy for answers, but she'd already moved on.

She was thinking about the quickest way to reach the summit. If they could avoid confrontation that would be better, as it would give them more time to look for the anchor uninterrupted, but if they had to fight, well that could be arranged too.

"We leave at dawn," she told them, then turned for the stairs leading to their rooms.

"But what if it's still like this!?" Jake asked. His reluctance to go back out in to the storm apparent for all to see.

Amy didn't turn or acknowledge his question, to which he was secretly grateful. The thought of a confrontation with her, when she was like this, was something he'd very much rather avoid.

As soon as she'd gone Jake, Billy, Nicolas, and even Issy breathed a sigh of relief.

"What the fuck is going on? What's wrong with her, and how does she know all this stuff. Who are *they*?" Billy's frustration tumbled out in harsh whispers. As frustrated as he was he was still careful to keep the volume down in case Amy could hear him upstairs.

"And what are we going to do about *him*?" Billy added, pointing unsubtly at Nicolas.

CHAPTER 15: NICOLAS

Nicolas looked at Billy who was a good twelve centimetres (five inches) taller than him, and considerably bigger in build. With his Giants shirt stuck to his broad shoulders and his face full of frustration and anger, Nicolas didn't fancy getting into a fight with this man—or doing anything that may risk bringing his friend back downstairs. She absolutely terrified him.

"I do know about the trail... and *them*," he began, hoping to dig himself out of a hole. "But I think we're on the same side."

"What do you mean?" Jake asked.

Nicolas reached into his pocket and pulled out his tobacco.

"Mind if I smoke?"

"Sure, if I can have one," Billy replied.

"Me too," Jake said quickly.

Issy rolled her eyes.

"Can you open the door a bit?" Nicolas said to Issy, adding, "Please." When he saw she was in no mood to take orders and looked like she'd happily stand up and punch him.

"What about... *them?*" she asked, hesitating.

"If they were going to attempt to get in they would have done it already," Nicolas said, trying to get just the right amount of tobacco on the tiny piece of paper. "And most likely we'd all be dead. Well, most of us," he added, lifting his head briefly to check Amy hadn't silently floated back into the room.

Satisfied she hadn't, he continued rolling. "It's not like them to come this close anyways. I mean it's not *unheard of,* and there have been skirmishes inland on various islands, including this one. But they're extremely rare.

"We think they like to keep themselves hidden; the more they venture on land, the more at risk they are of being discovered, that kind of thing. It's just a theory though," he added, oblivious to the growing confusion and frustration from Jake, Issy, and Billy.

They wanted badly to stop Nicolas and make him explain every sentence in more detail, but they also wanted him to keep talking. For the first time since they'd embarked on this journey they felt close to finally getting some answers.

"We call them storm hiders," he said through a mouthful of smoke. "For years they've loitered off the shores, waiting for the clouds to descend so they can use them for cover to get close and attack lone vessels out at sea.

"Mostly when they attack, after they've unloaded the cargo they came for, they kill the crew and sink the ship," Nicolas said flatly.

He ignored Billy, Jake, and Issy's horrified expressions. "Very occasionally they get sloppy, or interrupted, and they leave the shell of the ship floating on the water. But they never leave the crew. They're meticulous in that. We guess they're protecting their secrets, especially where they're from, and dead men can't talk, right?" he said, letting out a hollow laugh.

Nicolas sucked hard on his roll-up making the end burn a bright orange colour. Issy, Jake, and Billy stared dumbly into the smoke as it made its way out of his lungs and filled the air around them. They couldn't believe what they were hearing.

"You said they only attack during storms?" Jake asked finally, remembering how the sinister man with the grey beard had appeared just as the clouds had opened when they were in Barbados.

"Mostly." Nicolas nodded. "On the sea they use the mist and fog to hide their approach and get as close to their target as they can before being seen, giving them the advantage of surprise. They normally take merchant ships, often carrying fairly ordinary supplies such as food and water, or medical supplies, but they've seized higher value targets too—nothing seems to be off limits.

"Even when they venture on land it's usually during a storm. It's ironic really. We think they use the storms to stay hidden, but whenever the skies open up and thunder and lightning follows—we know they're coming." Nicolas snorted as he looked towards the glass door and the swirling wind and rain.

Jake took a drag on his now lit cigarette. He looked out at the path they'd arrived on earlier, just visible in the evening twilight, the wind bending and twisting the nearby trees, obscuring its location. He imagined a whole army of men, cloaked figures with dark beards, swirling hair, and cold, dead eyes lurking just beyond the lip of the hill they'd scrambled up not more than an hour ago, and shivered.

"There is another reason too," Nicolas said, making Jake jump. He put the cigarette to his lips and began his ritual of a few short puffs holding the end to the flame while the others held their breath waiting for him to continue.

"But it's just fisherman's tales," he added. "Some old salts believe the gods are on their side too," he said, letting out another derisory snort.

"They think the storm hiders have some sort of pact with the Caribbean gods, and that the gods conjure storms for them whenever they need them," he said, taking another drag on his cigarette, "And not just storms. They say the gods come to their aid in the form of the creatures above, and below the water too, all as part of this treaty that was signed centuries ago." Nicolas laughed mid-inhale, smoke catching in his throat, causing him to have a coughing fit.

When he regained his composure, water still streaming from his eyes, he sat back in his chair expecting his guests to find the stories just as farcical as he did.

But the reaction he got was quite different.

Issy and Jake went pale and Billy instinctively touched his side, reaching for the still unhealed flesh wound he'd received in Barbados.

"Why don't you go to the police?" Issy asked, wanting to inject some normality back into a conversation that was getting all too much for her.

"Someone from my family did, once, years ago. It was after they'd attacked a battered old passenger cargo ship filled with gold. The merchants thought the disguise would work, but somehow the storm hiders still knew what was on board. Anyways, it was attacked just up the coast from here." He waved his arm vaguely towards the garden, and the sea beyond.

"My uncle went to investigate when he lost contact with the ship's captain, not long after it had set sail. A few miles out he found the ship, dead in the water. He pulled up alongside and climbed aboard what was left of her. The bow was sunken low in the water and the sides looked like they'd been bombarded by rocks.

"What he found made him reach for the side rail and heave his guts into the sea.

"There had been no more than twenty people on board, they'd tried to make it look like they were on their way to pick up tourists with an empty vessel—and they were all dead.

"My uncle said it looked like a massacre. He said some of the bodies were..." he paused. "They looked like they'd been ripped in two, and he just couldn't understand what could have done such damage.

"With the gold gone, the crew dead and the ship heading for the bottom of the sea, my uncle quickly called the authorities wanting justice for his friends," Nicolas said.

He took the last drag on his roll-up smoking it right down to his fingers, before flicking the butt out into the rain that was still hammering hard into the glass door.

"And? What did the police do?" Jake pressed.

Nicolas paused and took a deep breath. "They thought it was him," he said finally, letting his words hang.

"With no other suspects and no witnesses, all they had was my deeply disturbed uncle, and a blood bath. They kept him for as long as they could but eventually had to let him go because of a lack of evidence. Everyone still thought he did it though. And they don't forget. That happened back in the sixties, but people remember something like that," he said.

"That's why you're out here?" Billy stated quietly, not really looking for an answer.

Nicolas just stared out at the rain.

"They started a resistance," Nicolas said, sounding downhearted.

"Who did?" Billy asked, trying to keep up.

"Other families that had been affected joined forces, and they chose my uncle as leader. After they discovered the ship massacre all the old myths about the storm hiders and the different Caribbean gods were dragged up, and superstitions went into overdrive.

"Many even fled the resistance because they believed any fight was lost before it had begun. They believed men who could call upon the gods of the Caribbean couldn't be killed—but my uncle proved that theory wrong at least," he said bitterly.

"Your uncle has killed one of them?" Jake asked stunned.

"We've killed around a dozen of them in total, they die just like any other man," Nicolas said.

No one knew what to say and Jake suddenly felt very far from home.

Nicolas reached into his pocket and took out his tobacco once more.

"Something strange is happening," he said. "About a week ago, everything started to change."

Billy flashed Jake a look. "What do you mean?" he asked, trying to keep his voice as neutral as possible.

"They seem less worried about coming ashore now, and more worried about something *else*.

"A lot of weird shit has been going on. I've seen your friend, so I know you are familiar with the concept. I imagine she's not always like that, no?" Nicolas said, looking at them for answers but finding only Issy staring angrily back at him. Billy and Jake remained quiet, hoping he would quickly move on.

"As I thought," Nicolas continued. "We are experiencing our fair share of irregularities here too.

"The animals on this island, and others, have become... unpredictable. I don't know. Maybe there is *some* truth in the superstitions, perhaps they do have a connection to nature somehow.

"There has been a big spike in shark attacks, we hardly get any in the Caribbean and we've had five in as many days."

Billy flinched and Jake and Issy tried to keep quiet. All three of them wanted to scream.

"The thing is one of the victims was a storm hider, which is a first. If they do have some agreement in place with the gods of nature, then it seems the gods are no longer keeping to it." He laughed bitterly.

"There have also been reports of lizards attacking bigger animals like sheep and goats, and even some humans, and the birds have been going crazy. Huge flocks of them have been seen screeching through the tree-tops and high above the cliffs scaring the locals with their unbearable shrieking.

"It seems the gods of nature are pretty pissed off," Nicolas said resentfully, flicking his second cigarette into the wind.

"How do you know about the trail? And where does it go?" Jake asked, remembering why they were there and feeling a need for more urgency.

"They go all over the island, and you'd never find them unless you were *really* looking.

"Apparently my family, and other families who'd had run-ins with these thieves made the trails so they could move around undetected and keep an eye out for ships on the horizon."

Billy and Jake listened intently to Nicolas. Issy had a glazed, far off look to her eyes.

"Anything that looked odd or threatening was flagged, and word spread across the island to warn merchants to alter their schedule or shipping routes. But the storm hiders found them, too, and started using them to identify their next targets and spy on the locals inland; see what they're up to.

"There were a few clashes with some of our men and their lookout. We only know because our lookouts never came back and were later found cut open and left in the mud. That's why we don't use the trails as much anymore, only when we really have to," Nicolas said. "And there are a few trails we think even they still don't know about."

"So, the trail going up to the cliff, that joins on to the path that goes to the beach from here, what's up there?" Jake asked.

Billy touched his arm and shot him a look. So far they'd managed to tell Nicolas almost nothing, and Billy wanted to keep it that way.

"Whatever you're looking for, it seems they want it too—and I want no part in it," Nicolas said, catching the exchange.

"Either they don't know where it is, and they need you to show them, which is one possible explanation as to why you're still alive. Or they're looking for it right now, maybe they've even found it. If it means things go back to normal—then I really hope so."

"Normal? You live in fear!" Issy snapped, deciding she really didn't like Nicolas. "You've been forced to hide away in this creepy little house in the jungle, scurrying around on secret paths, hoping no one sees you," she said testily.

"Maybe so, but it is better than ending up dead, which is where you are headed if you carry on your path. This has been going on a lot longer than you have. You have no idea." He gave her a dismissive look but was clearly rattled by her outburst.

Issy was about to weigh in again when Jake stepped in.

"It's been a pretty stressful day, to say the least. I think we're going to turn in and we'll be out of your hair tomorrow, at dawn apparently. We didn't mean to cause any offence and thanks for letting us stay here," Jake added.

Nicolas nodded.

Issy held her tongue, got up and walked towards the stairs without saying goodnight. She'd had enough for one day and hoped she'd find Amy in a slightly better mood than she'd last seen her in, and preferably more herself.

"Mind if I have one more?" Billy asked, not standing up just yet.

Nicolas raised his eyebrows ever so slightly then nodded, extending the nod to Jake too. "Please," he offered, passing the tobacco over.

Jake took the packet. He rolled a cigarette for Billy and handed it over, then rolled another for himself.

"How many have you seen?" Billy asked, smoke billowing from his nostrils as he handed the lighter back to Nicolas.

"Me? I've only ever seen one, and I've seen a few different ships out at sea," he said. "I've never caught them on a clear day, they've always been shrouded in mist—like I said we think they use the weather as cover—but from what I have seen it looks like they use old warships, like really old.

"I think it's all part of it. You know? They don't want to be seen, but if they are they want to scare the living hell out of people so much that they won't come looking. It works," Nicolas added, forcing out another cloud of smoke.

"You said you've seen one," said Jake. "Where did you see them?"

"On the trail you're looking for," replied Nicolas, staring out the window towards the jungle path.

"I was heading up to the cliff, I used to go up there all the time. I had a telescope set up on the top so I could look out to sea and keep an eye out for them—that's where I've been when I've seen their ships.

"Then around a year ago I was almost at the top. I could see where the trees thinned out up ahead and the sky widened but silhouetted against the bright blue backdrop I could see a man kneeling down on the trail with his back to me.

"There aren't many of us on this side of the island, and I know everyone by sight. This man was a stranger to me, which meant he was one of them.

"I froze, I didn't know what to do. If I turned and ran I'd no doubt make some noise and give my position away, if he didn't already know I was there. And I couldn't carry on. The trail's narrow. There was no way of getting past him without him seeing. So I stood as still as a statue, barely even breathing.

"The man stayed crouched to the ground, not moving a muscle. It seemed like forever but must have been no more than a couple of minutes. I remember wondering if he was dead he was so still.

"Then I saw him reach out his right hand and pick up his black wide-brimmed hat that I hadn't noticed was on a rock next to him.

"He placed it on his head neatly and rose to his feet. He was tall, broad-backed, with long, dark grey hair. I should have turned and ran then but I was paralysed by fear. It wasn't until he turned around and looked at me with those black, dead eyes that my body finally jerked free of his spell.

"I ran so fast I fell two or three times on the way back. I picked myself up straight away each time and I never, never looked back to see if he was chasing me.

"I thought my heart wouldn't take such pressure but somehow I arrived back here. I was sick in the garden just out there," Nicolas pointed.

"Did he have a grey beard too?" Jake asked.

Nicolas stared at him. His surprise faded quickly.

"You have seen him too," he stated. "He's hunting you?"

No one spoke for a few minutes while the three of them made peace with their own nightmarish visions.

"He enjoys it," Nicolas said finally.

"What do you mean?" Billy asked.

"I only saw his face for a second, and I was in shock, but I swear I saw a smile somewhere in those dead eyes, or I felt it. I think he knew I was there all along," Nicolas said.

The three of them gazed out the glass to the darkening rainforest. Jake stood up and slid across the door and locked it, having a sudden urge to shut out whatever was out there.

"Thanks, Nicolas," Billy said, handing back the tobacco.

"You're welcome. If I can't stop you, be careful. I have only shared a fraction of the stories about them with you, but I hope it's enough of a reminder to stay hidden at all costs. If they find you, it'll take more than just your friend to save you," he said solemnly.

CHAPTER 16: THE REPORT

The Watchman hesitated at Captain Sands' door back aboard the Devil's Liberty.

He'd been over what he was going to say a dozen times in his head as he'd made the return journey to his ship, but no matter how he spun it he knew what the likely reaction would be, and he was as nervous as the first time they'd met.

When Jonas Sands was first sent to the Caribbean from America by his father, it had been to preach Puritan beliefs across the islands, as were his father's wishes. But he'd had other ideas. By the time he landed in the Bahamas he had no intention of spreading god's word, or his father's, and saw an opportunity to start again.

He didn't believe in one god anyway, gods maybe, but none of that really interested him. He wanted to build a legacy. His dream was to create a state where everyone was valued. The spoils of war and labour would be shared among the people, and they would support each other in their toils, no one would go hungry, and in his mind that had nothing to do with god. Of course, this world would need a strong leader, someone to assign roles and ensure they were carried out correctly, and he really believed he was the man—more than a man.

The Watchman had been one of the first to meet him after word had spread as far south as Barbados that a rich American had newly arrived and was looking for a crew. They said he was a monster of a man, as wide as he was tall, skilled with his fists, and quick to judge, but if you were chosen you would be set for life.

He'd been freer with his talk back then, happy to share his grand visions for the world as a test, reading the reactions of the men who put themselves forward, and basing his verdict on how they responded.

The Watchman must have provided the required enthusiasm. The captain had come from behind his desk, slapped him on the back hard and put a big arm around his shoulder. They'd returned to the ship's deck together, and the captain had made a big deal of presenting the ship's new master tracker and huntsmen to the rest of the crew.

He doubted very much he'd receive such a reception this time.

Straightening his hat, he pulled himself up to his full height and knocked hard three times.

"Enter."

The Watchman pushed open the door and stepped inside the gloomy cabin. It was night outside and only a sliver of moonlight dared creep through the small window away to Captain Sands' right. The only other light came from two dripping candles, one on a shelf to the captain's left and one on his desk right in front of him, illuminating his large head and causing strands of his long, thin hair and untamed beard to form disturbing shadows on the wall.

The Watchman could clearly see he was irritated.

"Well?" he said impatiently.

The Watchman opened his mouth to speak but was cut off before he had the chance.

"Don't even bother. They're not dead, right?"

Again, the Watchman went to speak but was cut off by the captain, this time by holding one big hand up in front of the Watchman's face to stop him before he began.

"Fucking waste of time," he muttered under his breath.

A half-empty rum bottle at the corner of the captain's desk caught the Watchman's eye.

He's drunk.

The Watchman looked again at the captain, his eyes now more accustomed to the light.

Captain Sands was normally regimented in everything he did, including his appearance. But the Watchman could see now his hair was wild, his shirt unbuttoned almost down to where his big belly began, and he was ever-so-slightly slurring his words.

The Watchman sensed danger.

He's drunk. He's not waiting for a report he knows everything already.

Aware he had little time the Watchman started talking, prepared to ignore any commands to be silent. Under any normal circumstances it would have been an ill-advised gamble, but he had little choice.

"They have someone with them," he started. The captain ignored him and reached for the bottle on his desk.

"She's stronger than the others. It won't be as easy as we thought to kill them and…" the Watchman's words died in his throat as the captain threw the bottle at the wall spraying rum and glass across the room.

"There's something else…" he tried, panicking as Captain Sands got to his feet and started making his way around his desk.

Jonas Sands was far past his peak, but he was still a brute of a man. He'd always been good in a fight and even though age, ambition, and rum had covered his muscle in layer upon layer of fat it only seemed to add to his size advantage.

He closed the gap between himself and the Watchman in a flash and landed a big, righthand punch on the Watchman's left eye, almost knocking him off his feet.

The Watchman instinctively raised his fists, but it was too late. He regained focus just in time to see the captain's broad forehead rushing towards his face.

With an almighty crack, the Watchman's nose exploded. Pain shot through his body and he crumpled to the floor, blood raining from his injury.

* * *

Captain Sands stood over him swaying slightly, unsure whether his lack of balance was down to the rum or the ship, or both.

He sighed and reached down to pick up the limp body at his feet.

"I don't care who or what they have. They'll all soon be dead, same as you my friend," he said, heaving the Watchman over his shoulder then heading for the door to his cabin.

The deck of the ship was peaceful, and the crew were either fast asleep, or knew what was going on and were pretending to be out cold in order to keep themselves out of harm's way.

Captain Sands shuffled to the port side and without hesitation unceremoniously dumped the Watchman in to the sea.

CHAPTER 17: ALONE

The cold shocked the Watchman back to consciousness. He opened his eyes suddenly to find he was under water and sinking slowly.

As his memories came flooding back to him he remembered where he was, and what had happened. He couldn't understand why the captain had thrown him overboard instead of finishing him off. It was against their code to leave loose ends, and the captain had made the code—then realisation dawned on him.

He's going to let them finish me off.

It was common aboard the Devil's Liberty to allow the sea, and the monsters in its depths, to get rid of unwanted bodies. The Watchman had seen the captain dispose of many crews that way, and he felt ashamed as he thought of the role he'd played himself on more than one occasion.

He spun slowly, twisting himself around in the water in eerie silence, staring into the blackness around him unable to see a thing. Any moment he expected something to take hold of him and that would be it. He was terrified.

His only hope was the captain had been so drunk he'd forgotten all about him, and so had the sea.

He kicked his heels together propelling his body towards the surface.

It wasn't like the captain to leave things to chance, even if the odds were stacked in his favour, especially after what had happened on the island—but he had never seen the captain drunk like that.

Before the bubble of hope could rise, the hairs on the back of his neck stood on end and fear clasped hold of his body.

They're here.

Horror-stricken, he kicked his legs harder and thrashed his arms in front of him like he was trying to dig himself out from being buried alive.

Up above he could see the light from the moon through the sea's watery ceiling. He was almost there.

Just as his fingers were about to touch fresh air a huge dark mass pushed past him, clipping the right side of his body and sending him spinning into the side of the ship.

Adrenaline pumping and desperate for air he pushed for the surface again, bracing for another hit.

His right hand felt fresh air first, then his nose and mouth broke the surface. He choked and spat and tried to breathe all at the same time, causing him to choke and panic even more.

Realising his thrashing might be heard by the crew above, or worse the captain, who he pictured leaning over the side expecting to see a bloody feeding, he forced himself to stem his movements as best he could.

Taking short, sharp breaths he looked, pointlessly, around him. All was black. He felt hideously vulnerable with most of his body still submerged, and his arms and legs flailing beneath the waterline.

An excruciatingly slow minute passed without incident from above or below, and then another one.

He guarded himself against thinking he was in any way safe, knowing that any second a massive set of jaws could literally bite him in half.

For a moment the clouds parted, allowing more moonlight to fall on his surroundings. He thought he saw something, in the distance. The Watchman strained his eyes and scanned the gentle waves trying to rediscover the object that had caught his eye.

There.

A black fin was weaving its way silently through the water, and it was heading towards him.

Out of options and no longer caring about what noise he made, the Watchman turned and faced the Devil's Liberty, before manically trying to claw his way up the hull.

It was no use. He knew he'd never be able to pull himself up out of the water from where he was.

He closed his eyes, let himself sink and waited for the impact, hoping the shark would finish him in one go and not leave him horribly dismembered but still alive.

Trembling uncontrollably, he bobbed up and down in time with the waves, waiting.

He flinched as he helplessly imagined the massive fish ploughing into his midriff.

But nothing happened.

Where are you?

After the longest minutes of the Watchman's life, he forced his rigid arms and legs to move in the water once more, turning his body to face the direction of where he'd last seen the shark.

The moon was now full and bright, and he could clearly see the surface of the water for some distance around him. He scanned the waves urgently for any sign of a fin.

A few more minutes went by, and then a few more, and the Watchman, who began to tread water more fluidly, was unable to suppress the one emotion he'd least been expecting to feel given his situation—hope.

He thought about the rigger who'd been attacked a few days earlier after he'd fallen in the sea during choppy waters. A frenzy of sharks had gone for him as violently as any of their enemies, and none of them had seen that happen before.

The captain had brushed off the disturbing occurrence saying the rigger had been planning a mutiny, with no further explanation forthcoming. It didn't explain how *they* knew that. Could they read minds too? The Watchman had known the rigger well. He wasn't the ambitious type, and he was certainly no traitor.

The captain had lied, he wasn't sure why, but he was in no doubt something was disrupting the balance of things.

Maybe they've forsaken us.

Hope grew and filled the Watchman's chest as he quickly scanned the waterline. This time he wasn't looking for the shark—he was searching for land.

He knew they hadn't anchored far from shore, if he could just get his bearings there was a chance he could make a swim for it. But he'd need to be sure. If he ended up swimming miles out in the wrong direction, the sea would definitely take him sooner or later, no matter whose side it was on.

Taking one last glance back up at the ship, the Watchman began a steady breaststroke in the direction of the island he hoped was only a few miles ahead of him.

He had no plan, other than survival. For the first time in years, the Watchman's actions were entirely his own.

He swam on in the cold darkness, preying he wouldn't get picked off from below or dragged out to a certain drowning by a strong current.

Despite the very real risks of an imminent and ghastly death, the Watchman managed a wet smile through his now blue lips.

I'm free.

CHAPTER 18: ON THE RIGHT TRAIL

As the first rays of light hit the wet, sticky trail in front of him Jake couldn't help but marvel at where he was.

If someone had told him a few weeks ago, when he was still pouring pints in the Trow, and the grey British sky was endlessly emptying its bowels on everything outside, that he'd be hiking a hidden trail at sunrise in search of treasure, he'd have thought they were high.

They'd eaten a quick breakfast of cereal, a banana, and a coffee while it was still dark. Billy had insisted on the coffee and had even earned a half smile from Amy for his stubbornness on the point. Sensing an opportunity to find out a bit more from Amy regarding the plan for the day Jake had jumped in and asked for more details.

All she'd told them was that the trail led to the top of the cliff, and the anchor was up there. Then she'd finished adding items to her yellow backpack, including the Barbados bottle, as agreed, as well as a large knife from the kitchen of the guest house, before taking herself and her things outside to wait for them.

Jake had stuffed a few more bananas, a couple of spare t-shirts, which he'd carefully wrapped around the Antigua bottle and the hidden island bottle, and a first-aid kit he'd found in the communal area, in his roll-top backpack and followed suit.

They'd worried the storm would still be raging when they set off but, aside from a few broken trees and strewn branches and leaves, there was no sign of it.

The air was fresh but not cold, and as soon as the sun crept above the tree tops the rainforest jungle had warmed-up nicely.

Billy caught Jake staring up at the bright sky looking pleased. "So far so good, huh?" he said, knowing Jake was thinking about the storm hiders Nicolas had told them about.

"Not much to hide in right now that's for sure," Jake agreed.

The walk to the beginning of the hidden trail with the sun's warmth, the freshness from the rain, and the early morning air still present was a pleasant one.

"There," Amy said, pointing up ahead and off to the right.

Jake looked past her finger and saw nothing but jungle. He was sure she was right, but he couldn't see anything.

"Explains why we didn't find it before," he said quietly, half to himself and half to Billy just behind him.

Amy moved on ahead wading through the thick ferns, their leaves slapping her thighs as she pushed past them. She still managed to look glamourous in a pair of white chino shorts, trainers, and a black cropped t-shirt. She'd even found time to apply a bright red lipstick.

A few metres (ten feet) in and they could see the trail they'd been searching for. Jake looked along it as far as he could, and saw it wound its way upwards, deep into more jungle. He had no doubt this was where they needed to be.

"How long do you think it'll take us to hit the top?" Billy called up ahead.

Either Amy didn't know or didn't care to answer. She just marched onwards, eyes forward.

The others could sense her determination even from the back of her and drew comfort from the sight of her bright little backpack bouncing along up ahead of them.

Despite being unable to fully explain why Jake, Billy, and Issy all felt a lot safer with Amy in their ranks.

CHAPTER 19: DRIFTWOOD

The Watchman awoke with a start.

When he pried his eyes open, his vision was blurred and he blinked repeatedly, trying to focus.

His head hurt.

Finally, the blur moulded itself together into one complete shape and the Watchman had a clear view along a long empty stretch of beach.

He lay still for a moment, his senses on overload, as he tried to piece together where he was, and why.

It's morning.

The Watchman had a flashback of swimming in darkness, for hours, out at sea. His body convulsed as the memory of the shark, and then the captain converged on him hard.

Still grimacing he rolled to his left in the direction his head was facing and put his right arm down on the wet sand. He shook as he pushed himself into an upright sitting position, then scooted himself round slightly so his entire body faced along the beach, instead of looking out to sea.

He'd had enough of the sea. He'd been swimming and fighting the waves the entire night, and a good portion of the morning too. He didn't remember the last stretch, or how he got to the beach. He'd blacked out near the end and let the current complete the final leg of his journey for him. The Caribbean gods had decided, this time, to take him back to shore and give him another chance.

He could see a crab scurrying along a little ahead of him, dancing around some driftwood on its way further up the beach.

The Watchman followed it with his eyes, stopping himself thinking about anything else for a moment and allowing his shattered body to just get used to being conscious again.

When it had disappeared entirely from view he decided it was time to try standing. He thought it would be easiest to get up from his knees, so he lay back down and rolled over onto his front, before slowly forcing himself to his knees in a press-up position. He then brought one foot forward placing it flat on the sand.

Dragging himself to his feet he tested out a few steps and found his entire body was completely shattered. He dropped to one knee again, frustrated, and knew if he gave in to his tiredness he may never get up again.

After another huge effort to get himself upright he stumbled up the beach in pursuit of the crab, instinct taking him towards the trees.

Fire, and food.

The stumbling shuffle became less painful the longer he went, his muscles reactivating, and his mind determined.

He remembered how the captain had knocked him down on his cabin floor with ease, and he winced with shame.

I should have broken free a long time ago.

Bending down with great difficulty he started collecting the drier branches from the ground. Long used to taking care of himself in the wild the Watchman was usually a master when it came to foraging for firewood and setting up camp, but, battered and broken, he barely knew what he was doing.

After slowly stripping the branches of their wetness he placed them in a pile, added some shredded twigs and kindling he'd found, and reached for the magnifying glass from his coat pocket, panicking that he hadn't checked it was there until now and dreading it had fallen to the bottom of the sea.

His fingers touched its gold frame with the snake wrapped around it, its head poking up at one end, and he breathed a huge sigh of relief. He'd taken it off a merchant ship they'd attacked years ago and kept it with him to use as a fire starter ever since.

As a thin line of smoke made its way up into the air from the tiny but growing flames the Watchman allowed himself a short break. He knew if he stopped for too long he may as well have not bothered with the fire in the first place.

Over the years he'd realised that he could go longer and longer without sustenance, but even he had a limit. And after his body had taken such a pounding, first from the captain, then from the sea, for so many hours on end, he found himself closer to just giving in than he'd been in a very long time, and he'd had more opportunities to give up than most in his life.

The Watchman was a foundling; abandoned by his mother and left under a bush on Baltic Street West in London, he'd spent most of his childhood just surviving, running from one temporary sanctuary to another, taking shelter and food wherever he could.

He used to sit on the docks and watch the ships come and go, fascinated by the men and women who boarded them, and tempted by those who departed, sometimes resisting the urge to rob them but often hunger and, if he was honest, boredom got the better of him. It had even led to his first kill.

At twelve years old, an elderly well-dressed man had stuck out as an easy target, so he'd followed him, waiting for an opportunity to jump out and scare him. The Watchman had already endured a lifetime of horrors and he thought of himself as much older than he actually was. He also figured his feral appearance, and the dagger at his hip, would be more than enough to get the old man to hand over whatever he had on him.

He waited until the man went underneath a bridge he knew well before making his move—even back then he was careful when planning an attack. But the man hadn't been scared, as he'd expected, and he'd refused to give him anything. He could have walked away but backing down had never turned out well for him, and he'd learned turning your back in most situations was a mistake, so he'd attacked.

The old man had been stronger than he looked, and they'd wrestled on the cobbles for a good few minutes before the

Watchman managed to wriggle his arm free and drive his blade into the old man's stomach.

There had been so much blood it had scared him. He knew he'd done something terrible, something he could never take back, and as he stood over the dying man, the blood almost touching his battered shoes, he thought about taking the dagger and using it on himself. The moment eventually passed, and he'd found himself running once more, he didn't know where, just running.

The Watchman snapped himself from his trance and got himself upright with a loud groan, leaning against a tree for support. He had to keep moving. His hand reached to his waist and found his hunting knife and his dagger were both still with him, secured in their leather sheaths strapped to his belt.

Making as little sound as possible he strode carefully into the undergrowth, skimming the ferns for any sign of movement.

He was a skilled tracker and enjoyed being back in his element. Often in the past he'd get sent on to new islands first to identify potential threats and weigh up whether a particular beach was habitable, even for a short while, for the crew back aboard his ship.

That had been more before his time with Captain Sands though. Captain Sands had mainly used him as an assassin, and as a replacement for *him*.

The Watchman knew he'd never quite lived up to expectations, and despite being more skilled on land than anyone else in Sands' crew, he'd suspected he was nothing more than a mediocre tool to the captain, to be discarded as soon as it was deemed broken or a better means presented itself.

He'd been right.

Suddenly he froze. About ten metres (thirty-two feet) over to his left he'd seen something. His eyes scanned the area and he found the still shaking leaves, big enough to suggest whatever had passed through was of a meal-worthy size.

Another flicker of movement, this time a metre (three feet) closer to where he was standing.

Then another, and another, each ripple was in a direct line closer to his feet. The movements were more frequent and getting faster.

A branch snapped no more than three metres (almost ten feet) away.

It's attacking.

The Watchman pulled the single edged hunting knife from its sheath and raised it high above his right shoulder, his eyes tracking whatever was running at him from the undergrowth.

From virtually underneath his nose the head of a grey-green lizard the size of a terrier flew at his torso. Its eyes were wild and black, its sharp, narrow teeth were bared, and its surprisingly long claws were splayed and ready to hook into his flesh, in order to give it purchase to feed.

The knife cracked down on its skull while it was in mid-air, the blade forcing its way deep inside the lizard's head until it stopped moving and fell like a stone at his feet.

The Watchman took a breath. He wondered whether the captain knew he was here, and if more of these things were crawling through the ferns sniffing out his scent.

But he didn't think so. He cocked his head to one side looking at the creature with curiosity. It reminded him of the rigger, and the shark he'd encountered the night before. He shuddered again at the thought.

Unable to answer any of his own questions, he grabbed the lizard's thick tail, lifted the animal in the air and slung it over his left shoulder, before heading back to his makeshift camp.

The fire was still burning faintly thanks to the hot sun and shelter he'd built for it. He removed the lizard from his body and threw it down on the ground ready to be skinned and roasted.

He looked again at its thick tail, muscular arms and legs, and weighty body. It looked disgusting, but there was plenty of meat on it which could keep him going for a few days on the beach if he needed to stay put for a while.

Pushing his revulsion to the back of his mind he ripped and cut apart the lizard preparing it for cooking. Then he built up the fire as much as he could, knowing he didn't have the energy to do the job again if there was a lack of heat.

As the black smoke rose the Watchman was acutely aware that if the captain was looking for him, he'd now have a pretty good idea of his location.

But he had no choice. As soon as he was done he'd put the fire out, and hoped that in the meantime, if anyone was looking for him, they'd be looking in another direction.

CHAPTER 20: SMOKE

Jake wasn't sure how long they'd been hiking but he'd started to feel tired. He wanted to suggest a break, but Amy was still marching along up ahead. He could tell she was on a mission even without seeing her face and didn't dare to interrupt.

He glanced over his shoulder and gave Billy a look, but his friend was exhausted and could only shrug in response. His white vest and short-sleeved pastel yellow shirt were already soaking wet with sweat, and he looked like he'd been living rough for a week.

Jake decided to leave it for a bit longer and turned his focus back to the trail, hoping Billy would cave and ask to stop before he did.

As they climbed steadily, views of the coastline, the bays, and beaches dispersed along the edges of the island below them, had started to appear through gaps in the trees.

Jake could see the bright blue of the sea regularly cutting between branches and tree trunks as he walked along and kept watch to see if there were any hazy ships on the horizon.

He didn't really expect to see any, however. Not because he didn't believe in what his eyes had shown him, but because ever since Nicolas had told them that storm hiders only came when there was a storm, he'd felt safe as long as the sun was out.

He knew it was ridiculous to think that a nice day would prevent them being attacked, and he tried his best to stay vigilant and keep on guard.

He looked again to his left, searching the sea and the skyline for any dark objects or anything that looked out of place, checking the ground every few seconds to make sure he didn't trip up.

Mixed in with the clouds, not that far away from them, there was *something*. It wasn't a ship, but it still distracted him so much his right foot clipped the root of a tree and he stumbled, almost going over but catching himself just in time.

Rising up from a thick clump of trees Jake could see an unmistakable plume of smoke.

He kept his eyes on it for a few more steps, wondering who could be down there and whether he should alarm the others.

He reminded himself that it wasn't just them and storm hiders on the island. It could be anyone.

"Maybe it's just tourists camping. If it was storm hiders it'd be raining by now," he mumbled.

The trail took a sharp right as they wound around the side of the cliff, putting the smoke behind them. Jake didn't take his eyes away until he was walking forwards and looking back over his shoulder. By the time it became too much of a strain to look any longer, the smoke had all but stopped, making his mind up for him.

"There's no point telling them now," he said. "If I hold everyone up to look at smoke that *was* there but isn't anymore—that's not going to go down well."

He was entirely thinking about Amy. She was in an unstoppable mood, he just knew it, and there was no way he was going to hold her up for something so speculative. He convinced himself he was doing the right thing and decided to tell Billy and share the burden whenever they reached the top and he could steal a few moments alone just the two of them.

Jake looked up ahead to see how much further they had to go before they might reach a rest stop, only to see the trail weaving endlessly in a snake-like formation as far as he could see.

This could take a while.

CHAPTER 21: DANGER

The sea was calm and, well fed, the Watchman felt relatively content.

He had no idea what to do next, but the feeling was not an unwelcome one. Free of his shackles, he'd decided to do the one thing that hadn't been afforded to him, probably ever, in his entire adult life.

He sat and did nothing.

A few birds passed calmly overhead, and he saw another crab scuttle along the sand. The only unnatural animal he'd seen for a few hours had been the lizard, and all that remained of that was some bones and hunks of meat he'd chopped up and wrapped in leaves for later.

The lizard had made surprisingly good eating. The meat was relatively tasteless and reminded him of a chewier piece of chicken. Regardless, it had served its purpose and he'd felt his energy level rise.

The only thing he'd found wanting post his meal was some rum, and possibly a cigar.

As he sat by the still blazing fire he replayed events of the last few days and weeks over in his head.

Something on the islands had definitely changed, and by all accounts it had saved his life. He had his suspicions of what it was, and so did the captain. Someone was coming.

The captain had tasked him with casting a net and keeping a close watch. If anyone unusual surfaced he wanted to know about it, immediately. Then the Watchman had received a tip-off; four suspicious characters had been seen in Barbados, so he'd gone straight there. But as soon as he laid eyes on the four strangers he'd assumed there must have been a mix-up—they looked completely harmless.

He hadn't wanted to argue with the captain, he'd seen what had happened to those who had, so he'd proceeded as planned with every intention to kill them, no questions asked.

With the help of the resistance, and a great deal of fortune, they'd eluded him, and the Watchman had been reprimanded by the captain after he'd been forced to return empty-handed.

Given one more chance, the Watchman had been determined to put things right. He valued his position as the ship's chief lookout and primary assassin as it afforded him more freedom than anyone else in the crew. He was able to go wherever he wanted, providing he reported back regularly, and he achieved his objectives, and he didn't want to have that privilege taken from him.

He planned his second attempt much more carefully. As he sat on the sand he remembered how easily he had followed them to the Wild Bay Inn. The fact the resistance had helped them already rang alarm bells, but when they'd chosen to stay so far off the beaten track, and so close to the hidden trail, it only heightened the Watchman's suspicions. He had definitely underestimated them but was adamant he wouldn't do that again.

He had actually felt relaxed about it, and much more comfortable knowing they *were* a threat, and also very certain he was going to stop them.

That was until he'd seen her.

The confrontation with Amy, and the look she'd given him stalked his thoughts even more than being trapped in black water with sharks, or Captain Sands' cabin.

Aboard the Devil's Liberty he had tried to tell Captain Sands what he'd seen, but because he waited, unsure whether to divulge the information or save it for trading another time, Captain Sands had ignored his last words, assuming they were nothing more than a desperate plea from a condemned man, willing to say anything in order to save himself.

But he had seen something, *someone*, in Amy's eyes he hadn't expected to see, and in that moment he'd understood perfectly the threat this young, wild-looking woman posed.

Those weren't her eyes. They were *his*.

In the black depths of Amy's engorged pupils, the Watchman had clearly seen the Ghost.

Despite still being trapped and guarded, the Ghost was coming for them, and he was getting closer. When locking eyes with Amy he'd sensed more than just a threat from the Ghost too, he had been pleased, and as he thought back to the stare-off, the Watchman worked out why.

They were looking for the trail—and I showed them where it was.

If the Ghost wanted to find the trail, it must lead to something that could release him.

He knew now why the captain had been so on edge, and so hell bent on eliminating these four seemingly nobodies. The Ghost was probably the only thing in the world Captain Sands feared.

And with good reason.

The Watchman's trance was broken by something on the water. He only caught a glimpse of one of the masts, but it was enough to make his blood run cold.

Shit!

He scrambled to his feet and started kicking sand and dirt over the fire to put it out as quickly as possible.

Satisfied he had done as much as he could, he scanned the horizon again looking for his former ship.

Although he could no longer see any part of the vessel, he could see black clouds rolling towards the beach, and he knew they were there, and coming.

Suddenly a light fizzed inside his head.

He's not coming for me—he's coming for them.

It dawned on the Watchman why the captain had so easily disposed of him. He had already taken matters into his own hands.

He watched the storm build as the light faded along the beach.

His mind was buzzing as he played out events.

If the captain kills them—then he effectively kills the Ghost.

He envisioned a future where order was restored, and things returned to how they had been for hundreds of years—only in this particular future, the Watchman would be on the outside.

Unopposed, and without any loose ends to unravel him, Captain Sands would be free to roam and rule as he pleased, and the Watchman would have to live out the rest of his days in hiding, or worse. If they knew he was still alive, or ever found out, he would have to live in constant fear, always looking over his shoulder afraid, until one day one of the captain's men, or Sands himself, would finally catch him unawares and take him prisoner.

No!

He needed to act, fast. He needed to find them before Sands and his crew got to them first.

The Watchman checked his few belongings were intact and secure, certain he would need them, especially his knife and his dagger, very soon. Then set off into the jungle.

He had to get back to the trail and hoped to the gods they were still on it.

CHAPTER 22: STORM HIDERS

Amy stopped as the first rain drops filtered their way through the branches above them and slapped down hard on her head and face.

Jake stopped, too, causing Billy to almost walk straight into him. Issy saw the melee and looked up at the sky—and then to the sea.

Each of them looked worried, even, the others noticed for the first time, Amy, and none of them were surprised when a few drops rapidly turned into a deluge.

"Let's push on," Amy ordered.

Jake, Billy, and Issy weren't so sure hiking up an ever steepening incline in torrential rain was the best move. If conditions got much worse, and they hadn't found any shelter, they'd be completely exposed, and in more danger of being washed down the rocky hillside than anything else. At best they would have to start over from an unknown position, and at worst they might hit something hard and sharp on the way down and not be able to get up at all.

They pushed on for no more than five minutes before Amy herself slipped and landed knee first in the mud. The fall looked like it hurt, but either she hadn't felt it or refused to show she was in pain.

"Come on, Amy, we have to stop. This is ridiculous," Jake pleaded, as the rain fell harder than ever.

He looked around desperately for a place that could protect them from the downpour.

Amy could barely see the others the rain was falling so fast. She nodded, reluctantly, accepting they weren't going anywhere for a while. "Let's stop as soon as we find cover," she said.

As they struggled on, the weather became so intense the only thing each of them could focus on was putting one foot in front of the other.

The sky had blackened as dark as night, and the trail was illuminated only intermittently with each flash of lightning, making each step even more treacherous.

"There!" Billy cried out, pointing at a rocky overhang up ahead to their right.

Amy, Jake, and Issy looked to where he was pointing. It took them a moment but then they saw it too; an indent in the rock that looked like the entrance to a very shallow cave.

The violence in each blast of wind and the sheer volume of water pouring from the sky was enough to convince Jake the storm hiders had arrived, and he was sure the others were thinking the same. Heads down they hurried as quickly as they could up the final few steps.

One by one they crawled underneath the small overhang and pressed themselves into the rock at the back. The indent was just deep enough to fit them all in, but no one wanted to stay there for long.

"What's that?" Issy asked, pointing to something on the ground next to Jake's right knee.

At the base of the wall next to Jake, wedged into a gap in the rocks was a small plastic packet shaped a bit like an envelope.

Jake picked it out.

"It's tobacco, looks like Nicolas's. This must be a known resting place on the trail," he said.

The word *known* hung in the air.

"If Nicolas knows about it, then so do they. We can't stay here," Issy said, looking desperate.

"You're right. We need a plan. So, let's get thinking, and in the meantime—"

Billy took the tobacco off of Jake. "Is there a light in there too?"

Issy and Amy both looked like they were about to make a comment, but no words came, neither had the energy, and Issy was secretly glad of the distraction.

"You're unbelievable," she said, a tiny smile escaping.

"Don't worry, found one. It's in the packet, along with papers and even filters. I think Nicolas comes up here a lot more regularly than he let on," Billy said.

Billy faced the wall of the shallow cave and guarded his soon-to-be cigarette from the elements while he pieced it together.

Looking mighty pleased with himself he turned back to face the others, roll-up hanging between his grinning teeth.

It took him so many goes to light it that Amy eventually snatched it from him, put it in her mouth, popped her whole head inside her top and flicked the lighter once to produce a flame and inhaled until the roll-up burned brightly, before carefully removing her hands and head without burning herself or her clothes, taking a few drags as she did so.

"There," she said matter-of-factly, breathing out smoke and handing the lit cigarette to Billy, cupping the end so it wouldn't get wet.

Billy grinned, partly at getting his cigarette lit and partly at seeing the old Amy, if only for a moment.

"Right. Now that's sorted. Any ideas on what we're going to do?" Amy asked.

Billy puffed happily on his roll-up in the dry while the others chattered away, debating their options; their only option in fact—keep moving or go back?

"We're most likely half way to the top, or even closer," Jake said.

"You don't know that, but I agree going back is probably out of the question. I only said it because I can't think of anything else and wanted us to have at least one other choice. The trail may even have been swept away behind us, so we might not even be able to go back by now," Amy said, looking out at the rain.

Issy had never seen anything like it. She'd experienced big storms, and even Caribbean storms. She had been over to Jamaica once with her best friend from school who was Jamaican, and for three solid days the sky had erupted while she was there.

But this was something else.

Sheets of water were dropping off the ledge above them, smashing on to the lip of the cliff's entrance where they were sat. Thankfully most of the water splashed away down the slope, but there was still enough spraying back inside to make sitting there uncomfortable.

Billy turned his face away to preserve his cigarette.

"Let me have a few drags on that," Jake said. He took it from Billy's hand, keeping it covered.

"Okay. So, we wait here for a bit longer, then get moving again, I guess," Issy said reluctantly.

"We have to," agreed Amy. "We're sitting ducks here."

Jake passed what remained of the roll-up back to Billy keeping his last inhale of nicotine inside his lungs for as long as he could. He savoured the moment, knowing as soon as he let go of his breath it wouldn't be long before he'd be trudging through sludge again, and who knew what horrors lay ahead.

"What do we do if they're waiting for us on the trail?" Billy asked, flicking his cigarette butt into the gale where it was swept away and out of sight in a flash.

"We fight," Amy answered, as though it were obvious.

CHAPTER 23: AMBUSH

Before they set off again they'd prepped themselves for the bad weather as best they could, fully expecting it to last as long as the storm hiders were near.

Foraging around the mouth to the shallow cave they found a few sturdy branches which Billy had snapped into suitable heights for a walking stick, or weapon.

Jake and Issy had taken hold of their sticks gratefully. Amy had looked more sceptical, clearly thinking a branch wouldn't do any good against an army of storm hiders, but she'd taken it anyway.

They also made sure their shoes were secure so they wouldn't trip or have to stop and tie them, forcing everyone to stop and wait in the hellish conditions.

Finally, they agreed that if anyone saw another place to stop they should flag it immediately by placing a firm hand on the shoulder of the person in front of them, who would do the same to the person in front of them, until everyone had stopped.

The storm was loud, and the thunder and lightning were relentless, so it seemed like a good system. Plus, none of them wanted to alert the storm hiders of their whereabouts by yelling out that they'd found a good place to shelter.

Amy resumed her position at the front of the line, as was expected now by the others, with Jake following, and Billy, then Issy at the back. Amy kept hold of her yellow backpack and Jake fastened his roll-top securely to his shoulders.

Billy and Jake had tried to get Issy to swap places with one of them, and come in the middle, but she'd refused, pointing out that she was a much stronger climber than any of them. They couldn't argue with that and had resumed their places.

As they pushed on Jake tried to lift his head as often as he could from his feet, which took most of his focus. He knew he would slide all the way down to the bottom with just one slip, but he also wanted to see the storm hiders before they saw him, so he could warn the others and they could hide. What they would do then, he didn't know, but it panned out better in his mind than being taken by surprise and strangled in the rain. He'd never forget the look on the waiter's face in Barbados, when the sinister figure chasing them had picked him up by his throat and crushed his windpipe.

Jake looked down through the jungle tree-tops. He could still see a fair amount of the coast through the gaps, but the sea was totally obscured by a mass of black clouds. "A whole fleet could hide in there," he mumbled to himself as water dripped off his lips and chin.

A little further up to his left he noticed a bay he hadn't seen before; it looked like the trail would go right past it. They'd be able to look down at the sand and see if there was anywhere to hide.

He really hoped there was. The longer they walked the more it felt like they were heading into a trap.

He tried to give Billy a quick look to see if he'd spotted it too, but Billy's head was down and deep in concentration.

A few more minutes walking and the trail opened out on to a large clearing that reminded him of a roadside viewpoint, where people stopped to take pictures. A plateau jutted out towards the sea, with a steep drop off the edge, and a sharp rocky slope leading all the way to the bay below. On the far side he could see where the trail picked up again, weaving even higher up into the thick dark jungle.

As he stood in the gloom, looking over the edge as close as he dared get, the violent storm swirling all around him, he saw the entire bay light up as another flash of lightning tore across the sky overhead.

The beach was wilder and more overgrown than the beach near the guest house. The waves, whipped up by the storm, looked so angry they reminded Jake of rabid dogs, frothing at the mouth and hurling themselves on the shore, as though they sensed blood and were trying to get to the kill first. It brought back horrifying memories of their last time on the sea and Jake shivered.

Angular tall trees bent crookedly over each side of the beach, swaying so hard in the wind their branches were almost raking the sand. Large rocks lay unevenly along the shore with big pools of rippling water around them. Deep purple and black clouds were encamped overhead. The lightning ripped across the sky every few seconds briefly illuminating everything.

Amy brushed past Jake to get a better look, pushing her dripping wet hair behind her ears to try and stop it flapping around in the constant gale. Billy and Issy joined Jake, as afraid of getting any closer to the edge as he'd been.

They stood looking down at the steep drop.

"That's like the bay we found near the guest house, only with loads of creepy trees, big ugly rocks, and probably dead bodies buried under the sand. It looks like it's from a horror movie," Billy said. "Why are we stopping here?"

Jake gave him a look.

"Oh, no. No... no... no. I'd rather keep blindly climbing this never-ending trail than step one foot on Death Beach down there."

Issy was peering over the edge as close as she dared, enormous drops of rain cannoning off her face and body from all angles. "I can't say I'm that keen either," she said, raising her voice to be heard over the wail of the air rushing around them. "I'm not even sure we can get to it," she added, looking at the jagged rocks dotted across the steep descent.

"It'd take forever and there's a good chance we'll slip and fall, especially in this weather," she said, turning to face Jake to see how set he was on getting to the bay.

Billy did the same. "Come on, man, take another look. Does that scream safety to you?"

Just as Billy turned he felt something cold wrap itself around his ankle and grip him so hard it made him scream out in shock.

Issy looked to see what was happening and just as she saw the arm that had reached over the top of the ledge and grabbed Billy's ankle, another hand gripped her own leg and ripped her off her feet. She crashed to the wet ground hitting the muddy earth, knocking the wind out of her.

It had taken the storm hider that attacked Billy a few yanks to topple his heavy frame, his fingers slipping off Billy's ankles which were covered in slimy wet leaves and mud, giving Billy just enough time to put his arms out and brace slightly for the fall as he went over.

Lying face first in the dirt he looked down his body to see what had grabbed him. He caught a glimpse of a thick beard and zealous eyes before the storm hider heaved again, lurching him backwards another inch towards the edge of the plateau. Billy flailed his arms, reaching for anything he could hold onto to slow his momentum and take him away from whatever had hold of him, but the ground was water-logged and came away in his hands.

Issy managed to kick her attacker hard in his nose or jaw, or maybe his forehead, she wasn't sure, but she was certain she'd struck bone. Her leg was badly grazed and bleeding from where she'd been dragged and scraped across mud-covered rocks, but the adrenaline was blocking out the pain. She scrambled to one knee, and for a moment she thought she was free, only to feel the grip take hold of her even more firmly, wrenching her foot from under her again.

Jake darted forward to help, but Amy pushed past him, her face so full of empty death he stopped in his tracks and watched as she marched towards them.

Billy had rolled himself on to his back and was desperately trying to break free from the storm hider who now had a hold of both of his legs, and Issy, losing ground fast, was only a few centimetres (few inches) from the edge.

116

She screamed hard as her fingers lost their grip and she slipped again. Certain she was going over the edge, she saw Amy step past her head towards the storm hider still holding tightly to her calves and ankles, preparing for one final pull.

As Amy continued towards her feet Issy saw two more men levy themselves up and over the top of the ledge in the direction Amy had just come from, just behind where Jake was standing.

"JAKE!" she screamed hard.

Having waited for the first two to attack, the remaining two storm hiders had sprung up on the platform, intent on circling around the back of Jake and the others to make sure there was no escape.

He spun around to face them.

The storm hider closest to Jake was grinning. He was slightly shorter than Jake, but stockier, with a shaved head.

The second storm hider who'd appeared behind Jake was a monster. He was bigger than Billy, maybe even as tall as almost two hundred centimetres (six foot six). He had scraggly black hair and a large Roman nose. The expression on his face was completely blank.

Before they could advance any further a shrill, but unmistakeably male, scream of pure agony rang around the hillside, making each of them wince.

Amy had reached her victim. Without hesitation she'd lifted her leg as high as she could before bringing it down full force on the storm hider's left forearm. His fingers uncurled from around Issy's ankle and his scream continued to rise in pitch as Amy ground her heel down into flesh and tendons, and finally bone, until she'd crushed everything below her foot. With a final twist of her heel Amy lifted her now bloody white trainer, clumps of flesh, blood, and dirt dripping from the sole.

The storm hider dropped Issy's other leg and tried to scrape what remained of his left forearm off the ledge with his still good right hand. Anguish and pain turned to abject terror as he realised he

117

no longer had any purchase on the top of the ledge. He fell backwards still screaming, his bloody arm and limp swinging hand tumbling after him.

The screaming continued for another half a second before they heard an almighty crack and then nothing.

Issy scrambled herself away from the edge of the ledge shaking.

Jake looked back at his attackers who, despite looking less sure of themselves than when they'd first appeared after seeing what Amy was capable of, were still edging towards him. As it dawned upon him that there was a very real chance he wouldn't make it out of this alive, Jake spared a thought for the two bottles wrapped up inside his roll-top bag, still strapped securely to his back.

"It can't all be for nothing," he mumbled, edging backwards slowly, and preparing to fight.

Billy, emboldened by Amy's brutal retaliation had stopped digging for a handhold to claw his way further inland, and instead sat up and swung a big right hand at the wiry bald man who was clearly shaken after watching Amy maim his friend. The blow clipped the storm hider's rain-soaked temple, causing him to loosen his grip on Billy's legs.

Sensing Amy fast approaching he panicked and let go altogether, losing his balance in the process.

Amy gave the bald man's forehead a quick shove, which was all it took to completely dislodge him and send him tumbling down the steep slope. Billy heard a few dull thuds and then moaning seconds later. The storm hider might have survived the fall, but he didn't sound in a good way.

Amy stepped over Billy and advanced towards Jake and the two storm hiders still standing. The bigger of the pair took a step towards her, looking confused at how this eye-catching young woman had despatched two of his crew and was now squaring up to him, despite the fact he towered over her. The stocky shorter storm hider with the shaved head hurried closer to Jake, aware the time he had to complete his job was fast running out.

Before Amy could get within striking range, he had Jake in a headlock with a knife to his throat.

Issy and Billy watched helplessly. Amy's muscles twitched as she played out a variety of scenarios in her head, each ending in Jake's death—there was no way she could reach him in time.

CHAPTER 24: CHECKMATE

The Watchman had first found the four of them when they'd been sheltering.

He'd known Captain Sands and his men had been close because of the storm, and he'd guessed if the dark-haired woman and the others had set off on the trail in the morning, they would be in need of cover and would seek out the shallow cave. The Watchman had rested there a thousand times.

Keeping an eye on them from the shadows he'd given his position some more thought.

As he saw it he only really had two options, as returning to the Devil's Liberty and Captain Sands was out of the question. Even if he killed the dark-haired woman and the other three, and begged for forgiveness and his old position back, he knew it wouldn't work—he'd be killed on the spot and given another chance Sands would make sure this time.

The captain wasn't naturally a cruel man, but he was obsessed with control and wouldn't risk anything that might, later on, get in the way of his ambitions, and he did believe in setting an example. If a member of the crew started acting out and could no longer be relied upon to be predictable, Sands would become highly agitated, and whenever the Watchman had seen him like that a swift and brutal act had normally followed.

It was the captain's way of putting everything back neatly in the box he'd constructed, and the Watchman realised that's what the captain was currently trying to do too. The dark-haired woman and her friends were creating chaos in his order.

Sands' problem was that, despite his best efforts to act decisively, he still hadn't been able to regain control of the situation. He couldn't send his entire fleet ashore for risk of too much exposure. People would ask too many questions and an army of boats and planes would come looking. The Watchman knew Sands would never risk that.

So, he'd sent the Watchman, his best tracker and assassin, to deal with the problem quietly, only, again, it hadn't been that simple. Somehow the *Ghost* had been with them.

The Watchman thought back to his time working with the Ghost. He'd learned a lot from him, enough that Sands had seen fit to hand over his mantle when all hell had broken loose.

The thing he remembered most was his eyes, emotionless and cold in battle. He'd known straight away they were his when he'd locked eyes with Amy, they were unmistakable.

Another option was that he could join sides with them, with the Ghost.

He'd peered through the leaves of his hiding place and surveyed the group of four. The two young men had been sharing a cigarette, the blonde-haired woman had been more alert, constantly searching for signs of trouble outside, and the woman with the dark hair had sat still as a statue. She'd looked perfectly relaxed but also ready to strike at the first sign of trouble. The Watchman knew it was better to have someone capable of such sudden violence with you, and not against you.

He won't trust me.

The Watchman thought about how the Ghost might react if he presented himself and pledged his allegiance. Even without the added complication that he didn't know how much of the dark-haired woman was him, and how much remained of herself, he knew it would be difficult to convince the Ghost to trust him.

He could run. That was the only other option he could think of. The Watchman was no longer tied to anyone or anything, he had no obligations to fulfil, and could simply disappear, never to be seen again.

There were two things he found particularly troubling about this option. First, he didn't know what he would do. He'd never really had to think for himself, strategically, in terms of what he would do with his life, and the prospect was a daunting one. After a lifetime longer than most spent hiding, stealing, and contract killing, the thought of sitting on a beach for the rest of his days didn't fill him with longing.

Second, he'd be on the run, constantly looking over his shoulder. He didn't think Captain Sands would really follow him if he relocated himself on the other side of the world, but he was surely capable of finding and sending someone who would. And if the Watchman dealt with the first, he could send another, and another. Captain Sands was absolutely the type of man who wouldn't rest until proof was brought to him that the Watchman was dead, ideally in the form of his head. Captain Sands wasn't the resting type in the first place, he'd probably enjoy hunting him down—if he knew he was alive.

That was the real problem. He needed to know if the captain knew he was still alive. If he didn't, he decided to disappear. As daunting as the option was, it was better than being enslaved to the Ghost, even if he could convince him to trust him. He didn't know where he would go, yet, but he'd get a boat, something inconspicuous, and sail away.

He had a plan, but until he could gather more intel from the Devil's Liberty he needed an ally. He needed to get close to the Ghost, gain his backing as much as he could, and buy himself some time. Once he was certain the captain had already mentally buried him, he'd know he was free, and he could disappear. If it turned out the captain *was* coming for him, as well as the dark-haired woman and her allies, he'd stick with the Ghost for as long as he needed to.

Happy with his scheme the Watchman had continued to track Amy, Jake, Issy, and Billy, knowing that the crew of the Devil's Liberty were also on their trail.

He'd hidden in the shadows waiting for an opportunity to present itself, suspecting the clearing with the plateau would be where his former crew would choose to launch their attack, and making sure he was as close as possible.

When the Watchman saw Issy hit the ground he'd seen his chance, allowing the battle to play itself out a little in order to wait for the perfect moment to seize his opportunity.

As he'd expected, the Ghost had come to the fore. He'd seen the way Amy had mutilated Charles, inflicting maximum pain and instilling fear in those still standing. He'd seen the Ghost do it dozens of times before.

Tobias had rushed at Jake and pressed his knife to Jake's throat. The Watchman had known he was more than capable of finishing the job, but he had also known Tobias was far from a trained killer—and his hesitation was exactly what the Watchman had been waiting for.

He sprang from the nearby ferns and covered the distance between himself and Tobias in a few rapid strides just as a particularly bright flash of lightning crackled overhead.

When Amy saw him, she let out a scream that was more like the roar of a wild animal. The Watchman felt his stomach twist at the noise, but forced himself to block it out, hoping his gamble would pay off.

With his right arm he reached around the back of Tobias and clasped his hand over Tobias's wet fist clenching the knife, before skilfully easing it away from Jake's throat. With his left hand he stabbed the blade into the side of Tobias' chest, retrieving it and plunging it back in just below his first mark, deeper the second time with a sharp twist to make sure.

Tobias dropped to the ground, blood spilling from his stab wounds, mixing with the rainwater. The Watchman took a step back, knowing what happened next was largely out of his control.

Jake shuffled away from the Watchman, and Billy and Issy did the same from Amy and Leonard.

Amy glowered at the new arrival, completely ignoring Leonard, who looked thoroughly agitated. Suddenly he forced his enormous legs to the lip of the ledge in a couple of ungainly strides and threw himself off the edge, slipping on the wet rock at the last,

123

cutting short his leap and plummeting down just inches from the cliff face.

Inside his head the Watchman screamed in frustration. If the captain had thought he was dead, he soon wouldn't if that big idiot managed to survive.

He needed to make sure he died and wanted to rush to the edge of the ledge to check on his landing but couldn't take his eyes off Amy. He could track Leonard down to the beach, if he was still alive, and hopefully cut him off before he got word back to the Devil's Liberty.

Looking at Amy he read the Ghost's eyes, and quickly saw the Ghost was out of patience and about to unleash in his direction.

All or nothing.

Careful not to step forward or show any movement that could be interpreted as a threat, the Watchman slowly pulled his feet together, straightened his back, and bowed, his head so low to the ground his wet dripping hair grazed the mud. He had deliberately taken his eyes off of the Ghost and left himself completely vulnerable.

For a second or two nothing happened. Issy, Billy, and Jake stood watching in absolute bewilderment, while Amy smouldered, and thunder rolled overhead, noticeably a bit quieter than before.

All four of them waited for the Watchman to straighten himself up, which he eventually did, taking his time to really make his point.

Amy waited until he'd stretched his spine to its full length and was looking at her face again before she made a lunge for his throat with her right hand.

The Watchman just managed to dodge her grasp, her red nails touching the collar of his shirt as he jumped back. Anger etched across her face, she advanced again, pushing him towards the ledge.

The Watchman wanted to look behind him to see how far the fall was, and if he could see Leonard, but he knew he couldn't risk it. The Watchman changed his stance and braced himself.

"WAIT," Issy yelled giving both pause, just for a moment.

They didn't look at Issy, but they waited for her to talk.

"Amy wait. He… he saved Jake's life," she stated.

"He also tried to kill us if you remember," Billy hissed.

"I've seen enough… death," she said shakily, still picturing the storm hider's petrified face, and mutilated arm, flailing back from the ledge before his skull had cracked on a rock.

"Please, just stop," she begged, exhausted.

Amy faltered, her face showing subtle signs of softening. Issy had gotten through. A few more seconds passed before her rage evaporated, and she almost forgot the Watchman was still standing there.

She turned her back on him entirely and walked over to Issy, who saw her eyes had returned to normal and were no longer swollen and black, just full of tears.

She slumped to her knees and put her arms around Issy's neck, sobbing awkwardly into her shoulder.

Jake and Billy kept their eyes on the Watchman, not sure whether to fight, or to thank him.

Unsettled by the Ghost's sudden disappearance and the re-emergence of Amy, the Watchman nodded his subservience once more.

CHAPTER 25: THE SHELTER

"Are you guys okay?" Billy asked Amy and Issy. For the moment, they were just the four of them.

The rain had slowed to more of a drizzle and the clouds had changed to a lighter shade of grey.

Amy bit her lip hard and forced herself to keep a lid on things, determined not to let the swirling emotions overwhelm her completely. She stood up and paced the length of the plateau to keep herself busy, while Billy and Jake helped Issy to her feet and did their best to clean up the cuts and grazes on her legs, none of which were thankfully too deep.

"What the hell was that all about?" Billy asked, once he was sure they were out of immediate danger.

"I don't know, none of it makes any sense. One hundred per cent that's the same guy that stalked us in Barbados and had our waiter by the throat.

"And now he turns up here, jumps out from behind some bushes and saves my life," Jake said, crouching down on his toes with his knees bent. He stared up at each of them searching for answers.

"They were storm hiders, weren't they?" Issy asked.

"They definitely looked like Nicolas described. He's seen one, once, in his entire life, and we somehow run into a whole gang of them," Billy said, shaking his head in disbelief.

"Where did he go?" Jake asked, still crouching on the ground. "I mean, why save my life if you're just going to disappear straight afterwards?"

"You could ask him," Amy said quietly. Her face was pale, and her mascara had smudged around her eyes from crying.

"I would if he…" Jake trailed off, following her eyeline and realising the Watchman was behind him.

He whirled around so quickly he almost fell over. The Watchman was standing in the exact spot he'd first appeared, this time his arms were full of branches.

No one moved.

"Wood, for a fire," he said in a gravelly but not unpleasant voice. "There's another shelter just up ahead," he added, nodding to his right over to where the trail continued, his dark, wet hair swirling and sticking to his face.

"We're not seriously going to follow this asshole, are we?" Billy said, looking to the others.

Jake and Issy didn't speak. The Watchman had chased them, and he'd looked like he'd wanted to kill them in Barbados. But maybe they'd been mistaken. Maybe he'd been trying to save them all along. There was no denying he *had* just saved Jake's life.

Amy seemed to be entirely herself again and she wasn't interested in following the grey bearded stranger in the slightest, but she did want shelter. She was exhausted and close to passing out.

"I don't know, he did save my life," Jake said. "Maybe he knows something that might help us." He gave Billy a look.

The situation was surreal, and he felt absurd having the conversation with Billy while the Watchman himself was clearly listening, but he could see no other choice. He didn't want to fight that was for sure and worried if they just tried to walk off the Watchman would attack and stop them, or worse—which left only one option. He resigned himself to the fact going with him was the best they had.

He looked at Billy and shrugged slightly so Billy saw. It took him a minute, but Billy eventually got Jake's point just as he was coming to the same conclusion. "Okay. But just until we dry off," he said.

Issy nodded. They were in no state to protest and had to assume the Watchman was telling and not asking. She prepared to move by relieving Amy of her yellow backpack for a bit and, worried she might faint, she put an arm around her waist for support.

"Okay. Where are we going?" Jake asked the Watchman, signalling they were ready to follow.

Without a word the Watchman picked up the trail on the far side of the plateau and marched back into the jungle. Jake followed first, with Billy and Issy propping Amy up behind him.

No more than ten minutes back on the trail the Watchman stopped and turned to face them.

"This way," he said, veering into thicker jungle off to their right.

After twenty minutes of walking frustration and panic grew.

"Where is he taking us?" Issy hissed.

"I don't know, keep an eye out for a route out of here. If we see an escape, let's take it," Jake whispered back, making sure Billy had heard him too. He was worried his instincts had been wrong, and if anything happened to them, it was on him.

Amy's shoulders slumped and her head lolled. She was in need of a rest, some water, and something to eat. Billy and Issy knew she would collapse if they let go of her. Through a series of looks and whispers they agreed Billy would take her on his shoulders as soon as they could make a run for it.

Just as Jake thought he'd spotted a possible escape route the Watchman threw the branches he'd been carrying down in a pile on the ground.

He looked up ahead to see what had caused the Watchman to stop and saw an enormous tent behind him, wedged in between two large trees, constructed from what looked like the cloth of a ship's sails.

"Well, that's—unexpected," Billy said, almost lost for words.

The Watchman turned and removed some rocks from the base of the fabric, before folding the canvas up on each side and somehow pinning it back to reveal its interior.

Inside was big enough to easily fit all five of them, and the cloth had even been folded and separated with rope and strategically placed branches to create two separate rooms. In the bigger room to their right was a hammock swinging freely in the breeze, the storm having all but died out completely. And in the room to their left there were barrels, tins, and crates.

"What's in there?" Billy asked, suddenly starving.

The Watchman disappeared into the supply room, fetched a few empty crates from the back and ferried them across into the room with the hammock. After two more trips he'd set up five make-shift seats and busied himself in getting a fire going.

"Sit down," he said, trying to sound unthreatening, fully aware what they must be thinking.

Billy went first, leaving the crate furthest from the opening free, presuming the Watchman would want to sit on one of them. He wanted to make sure no one was boxed in and they could all still easily flee if it came down to it.

Jake, Issy, and Amy sat down on the crates that had been placed next to Billy. Despite the high probability they were still in danger, their bodies were broken, and they couldn't help but feel a huge relief at the weight being lifted from their feet.

The Watchman continued to build the fire close enough and big enough so that they would feel the benefit later on and he'd be able to cook for them, but just far enough away from the tent opening to keep the smoke outside.

"What is this place?" Jake asked him.

Without turning around the Watchman said, "When the islanders started using the trail more I built this shelter. I couldn't use the shallow cave anymore."

Jake and the others waited, but no further information was forthcoming.

"Rest, and then we'll eat, and then we'll talk," the Watchman said, sensing their frustration without needing to look at them.

Issy studied her surroundings more closely.

The room they were in was evidently the Watchman's bedroom, whenever he stayed there, and she couldn't help but be impressed with the condition he kept it in.

The ground had more cloth on it, and also layers of something else, some sort of sacks she thought but couldn't make out the material. It looked and felt like it had been painted with something too. Whatever it was it seemed to do a good job of keeping the water and damp out.

The ceiling itself looked like it had been reinforced and covered too. The cloth was patchy black and although there were drips of water creeping in via a few weak spots, the drizzle was largely kept at bay, and the tent, on the whole, was surprisingly dry. Issy was amazed the thing was still standing after the most recent storm; and sitting in a dry, relatively comfortable tent in the jungle was just unreal.

She looked over at the Watchman. He was busy stretching one of the cloth openings of the tent further out into the forest so it would cover the fire, just in case the rain started to pour down again. Then he knelt down, took something from his pocket, and bent forward so his face and hands were as close to the pile of wood as he could get. After around five minutes he cursed, stood up and went next door to rummage around in one of the tin containers. Returning promptly, he knelt next to the fire once again, this time pulling a small silver metal petrol lighter, flicked it to life and lit his fire first try.

Once it was burning he awkwardly sidled passed Issy and Amy, who were closest to the door, and sat on the crate at the back of the tent room.

Jake and Billy looked at each other, Issy held her breath, and Amy still looked like she might pass out.

The Watchman had been staring at Amy since he'd sat down. He stood up and took one step towards her. In unison, Billy, Jake, and Issy leapt up to their feet to stand in his way.

The Watchman held his empty hands up in the air to show he meant no harm. "She needs to rest, properly. Lift her into the hammock," he said, pointing at his bed in the corner.

As uncomfortable as each of them felt lifting Amy into the bed of a man who'd once tried to hunt them down and kill them, it was painfully obvious she needed to lie down.

Hoping their actions wouldn't come back to haunt them they helped her into the swinging canvas as carefully as they could, and within seconds of being horizontal she fell asleep.

The Watchman had remained sitting, allowing the others some space. Satisfied there was no hidden trap, and Amy was safe and comfortable, they each returned to their crates.

"Is this where you live?" Billy asked, breaking the silence, unable to keep the disbelief out of his voice.

"No…" The Watchman answered unconvincingly, realising as he answered he no longer had a home, and this makeshift shelter was as good as anything he did have.

Another long pause.

"I'll tell you what you want to know, and then you will tell me about her," he said, looking over at Amy who was sleeping soundly, oblivious to what was going on around her. "And what you are doing here."

CHAPTER 26: REVELATION

The Watchman had taken his time building the fire for them and setting up camp to give himself time to think. He'd been contemplating how much he should tell them, and how much he should leave out, not wanting to give away any crucial piece of information that may come back to haunt him later.

Jake had been doing exactly the same and they'd agreed to let him do the talking.

"I don't know how much you know about... us," the Watchman stated. "We've been around a long time, a lot longer than you might imagine."

Issy thought he looked in his late thirties or early forties and didn't really understand what he was talking about.

"The group that's hunting you, and they *are* hunting you, go back a long way, and they weren't always..." He struggled to find the words. "They weren't always what you see now.

"They're a unique colony, made up of all kinds of people, rich and poor, young and old, all with one thing in common, they were all searching for a way out.

"When the captain found them, they were tired of the disorder, the filth, the politics, and the constant back-stabbing. He gave them renewed hope—in the beginning anyway."

Jake noted the Watchman kept using 'they' instead of 'we.'

"Many of us had fled our countries once before, on a promise of freedom and a new life. That hadn't been easy. When we arrived in our new world, we wanted to make it work, even though, to those who wanted to see them, the cracks were there from the start.

"There were too many voices, too many egos for the Republic to thrive. It suited those used to taking things by force, with constant power battles at the top and complete lawlessness in the streets. It wasn't the *free* paradise we had been dreaming of, just another version of hell," The Watchman said bitterly.

Jake had been rapt on every word. He knew his pirate history inside out, and he suspected the Watchman was talking about Nassau, and the Pirate Republic. He stared in disbelief, thinking the Watchman must be out of his mind and, at the same time, wondering if there was any way his words could actually be true.

"The captain had believed in its ideology, but he'd been one of the first to argue more order was needed for the new world to truly work. He'd raised his concerns to the Brethren, but they were shot down—too many rivalries, and men just wanting to maintain their power.

"That's when he began recruiting," the Watchman said darkly. "He promised those that joined him the chance to live the life they'd all been promised, in peace and order, everything the Republic had failed to deliver.

"He wanted to build a fleet of warships, all centred around his own ship, the Liberty Pioneer. Once his fleet was of a size he was happy with he planned to set sail and find a new land of their own.

"But keeping his plan a secret wasn't easy. Many men were still too enamoured by the life of gluttony and debauchery that they'd made for themselves, even though it was going up in flames around them. They also didn't believe, or didn't want to believe, bigger and stronger powers overseas were planning to squash them and wipe them from existence.

"Those who refused the captain's approach then knew too much, and needed disposing of, quietly, if his plan was to remain a secret," he said, getting up.

The Watchman went next door. They heard him rummaging in one of the crates and then the unmistakable sound of bottles clinking together.

"Are you buying this?" Billy whispered to Issy and Jake.

"Some pretty strange things have happened to us on this trip." Jake shrugged, non-committal. He was desperate to hear the rest of the story.

The Watchman returned with two open bottles, one rum and one gin, and he also had a small box underneath his armpit. The bottles were around the same size as the bottles they had stowed in their backpacks, which made Jake's heart race, but relaxed when he saw they were nowhere near as old.

He handed them to Jake retrieving the box as soon as his hands were free and placing it on the ground in the middle of the group. He took the bottles back from Jake and put them on the makeshift table in front of everyone.

No one moved for a moment, then Billy reached forward and took the rum. "Fuck it," he said, taking a large gulp and swallowing quickly.

Jake followed suit and took a swig of gin before replacing the bottle on the table, trying hard not to screw up his face at the taste as he did so.

The Watchman sat back down and readied himself to resume his story, his face illuminated by the fire as the light faded outside.

"Captain Sands became impatient," he said, reaching for the bottle of rum Billy had drank from. "He worried he'd never be able to build a crew in secret, fast enough to see out his ambition.

"He'd wanted to cherry-pick the best of the Brethren, along with a few others outside, making sure he had the skills and qualities in all the right areas of his fleet in order for it to prosper elsewhere. But the slower his progress, the lower his standards dropped. Ambition outweighed all else, and he started targeting the outcasts, knowing there lay a higher chance of success, and disposal, should it be necessary, would be far less difficult.

"He told himself that, with stronger, singular leadership, any bad apples in the barrel would fall in line, and if they didn't he was prepared to deal with them. All that mattered to him by that point was making his vision a reality, at almost any cost. He was completely consumed by it," the Watchman said, remembering how his former captain had paced the deck day and night talking of nothing else.

"Even after he'd changed his selection criteria, and acquired dozens of men, things still weren't happening fast enough. News had arrived that government forces were taking action and were ready to wipe out the Republic. Not knowing how long he had, he recruited someone else too," he said gravely, glancing over at the hammock.

"He abandoned trying to persuade people through promise and reason and decided to use force and fear instead.

"He knew of one captain who'd refused to join the Brethren and was hated by them for it. He was a skilled sailor and master tactician in battle, often taking down entire ships without losing a single man.

"He became so good at surprising his enemies, raiding their ships and then disappearing without leaving a trace, that his assaults became infamous across the West Indies, and he became known only as the Ghost," he said, glancing again in Amy's direction. The hammock was still, but he needed to be careful in case she wasn't sleeping at all and was secretly listening.

He'd decided not to voice his theory about their friend until he was certain, and maybe not even then. It was the Ghost's support he needed, not theirs.

"He was ruthless," the Watchman continued. "Feared throughout the Caribbean, and almost impossible to track down. It took the captain months, but eventually he discovered the Ghost's stronghold in Saint Lucia, it was the one place he most called home.

"The Ghost knew the captain was looking for him and, according to the rumours, he was curious, and even flattered by the lengths Jonas had gone to in order to arrange a meeting—which is why when the captain pulled into the small bay where the Ghost had set up camp, he was met without hostility.

"The captain had been prepared for a fight, but when their boat was close they'd been helped to shore and guided along the beach by the Ghost's crew with flaming torches. The Ghost and the captain had disappeared somewhere inland, presumably to discuss terms in private.

"The closest of the captain's crew, including myself, sat on the sand and waited," he said, reaching for the bottle of rum again.

Jake's ears had pricked when the Watchman had said he was on the beach, himself. That he was actually *there*. If what he was saying was true then he really was a lot older than they were, like three-hundred-years older. Jake stared hard at his weather-worn face and dark eyes.

"It's impossible," Jake thought and nearly said out loud.

"After a few hours the Ghost and the captain returned, looking like a pair of sea dogs who'd known each other for years. Whatever the captain had told the Ghost had gone down well because we opened the rum after that, and both crews stayed on the beach and drank until they couldn't stand."

"What was the Ghost like, I mean up close?" Jake asked, curiosity prevailing over his scepticism.

The Watchman forced himself not to look at Amy again, and measured his words carefully.

"The Ghost just knew who, and what, he was and let it be," he said, the last few words with enough frustration in them to make Issy suspect he wasn't just talking about the Ghost.

"He wasn't as big as the captain physically," he continued. "But few men were. The Ghost was strong enough though, muscular and more agile—he was the captain's junior by around fifteen years. He had a brown beard, and short brown hair smoothed back over his head.

"He kept himself to himself, mostly, never saying more than a few words at a time. I remember him as quiet and observant, when he wasn't at arms, of course," the Watchman said. "In a fight, he was deadly. If there was a more efficient man or woman with a blade, or without for that matter, then I never met them."

What he really remembered most about the Ghost were his black emotionless eyes, especially just before a kill. He remembered the fear on the faces of the condemned—and, more than anything, he remembered the look the Ghost had given him that day on the beach, when he was tied and bound, covered in blood, and simmering with silent rage.

This time he did look over at the hammock, half expecting Amy to sit suddenly bolt upright and turn those big black pupils in his direction. Instinctively, he reached for the bottle.

"So, what happened?" Jake encouraged, taking the bottle directly from the Watchman, ignoring Billy's apprehensive look.

"The Ghost became part of the captain's crew," he said. "We often wondered what the terms had been, to get the most feared man on land or sea to take orders gladly, but they were never revealed to us." The last sentence a barely audible whisper.

"He became the captain's right hand man, and the two of them set about accomplishing the captain's grand ambition, an alternative to Nassau, a cleaner, more ordered, better new world.

"With the Ghost alongside him whole ships disappeared, then quietly reappeared at the side of the Liberty Pioneer, their crews and captains pledging their allegiance to Captain Sands, and no one else any the wiser. Blame fell on tropical storms and angry gods. No one suspected a thing, the Ghost made sure of it.

"When the captain's fleet was almost at the size he'd envisioned he returned to cherry-picking, sending the Ghost on more select missions to either scare the outstanding few on his list into submission, or kill them if it was clear they could never be trusted." He paused, eyeing the cigarette Billy was rolling from the packet of tobacco they'd found in the shallow cave.

"You smoke?" Billy asked, catching the Watchman staring at him as he pulled apart the pinch of tobacco he'd placed on a rolling paper to even it out.

The Watchman nodded and Billy passed the packet over. He expertly rolled then used the same petrol lighter he'd used to start the fire to light his cigarette, before passing it over to Billy.

The Watchman breathed the smoke in deeply and closed his eyes, then continued, "Everything had gone to plan. The captain had the following he wanted, and he had the Ghost by his side. They just needed somewhere to settle, a new island, untouched by man."

The Watchman dragged hard on his cigarette, then exhaled the smoke as slowly as possible.

Jake guessed the next part was either hard to explain, or extremely painful to tell.

CHAPTER 27: THE BETRAYAL

"The night before we were to set sail on our expedition—something happened. The captain, and a few select members of the crew, including myself, were invited to the next biggest ship in the fleet for a meal. It was meant to be a celebration of all we'd accomplished, and to toast our voyage in to the unknown, in search of the brightest of futures.

"The Ghost," his voice automatically went down a notch. "Wasn't among us. The captain of the Red Privateer couldn't bear to be in the same room as the Ghost, he said, because he didn't trust him, but more likely he was afraid of him like most men. He'd told the captain to leave his guard dog at home.

"The captain, not wanting to upset either his chief assassin and the head of his army, nor the captain of his second most powerful warship and commander of his fleet, had to tread carefully.

"He chose to give the Ghost full disclosure, telling him exactly what Captain Jones had said about him, and telling him not to worry about his words as the captain gave them no weight where the Ghost's position was concerned, but it would be best if he remained on the Liberty Pioneer all the same.

"The Ghost looked far from pleased, but he didn't object, and the captain went to the banquet.

"Wine and rum flowed, and dreams of how best to craft the first settlement when they'd agreed upon an island were shared. Captain Jones was adamant the new country should be easy to defend. His primary concern wasn't that we wouldn't be successful in our venture, but that we'd create something so much better than anyone else had that, when it was eventually discovered, the rest of the world would go all out to try and take it from us.

"That prompted some heated discussion which was instantly forgotten when Lewis, a gunner from the Liberty Pioneer and Captain Sands' crew, burst through the door barely able to breathe, soaking wet and covered in blood.

"He caused a hell of a stir making his way to the captain, struggling to walk straight, and smashing into the tables and the people more than once.

"Eventually able to catch his breath, and close enough to the captain to deliver his news he said the Ghost had lost his mind, and had marched through the Liberty Pioneer, slicing left and right until no man was left standing.

"Lewis had been behind his best friend when his friend had been struck across his throat, blood spattering Lewis's face and clothes. With the taste of hot blood still in his mouth he'd staggered backwards and fallen in to the sea.

"He'd swam for his life, desperately trying to reach the Red Privateer, knowing it was likely he was the only survivor, that he needed to raise the alarm.

"Exhausted but in one piece he'd made it," the Watchman recalled. He stared into the dark jungle beyond the fire and sighed. Jake could tell he wished the gunner had been lost to the sea.

"The captain couldn't believe it, but Captain Jones seized his opportunity. He said he warned us about the Ghost, that he was nothing more than a wild animal, and said we were wrong to invite a wolf to the dinner table.

"The captain, with Lewis collapsed at his feet soaking and bloody, was unable to argue. He'd been backed into a corner and worse still, he'd been embarrassed. He couldn't stand having the men he'd recruited, the captains he'd hand-picked and coerced into joining *him* on this expedition, standing over him telling him, to his face, that he was a fool.

"Needing to shut them up urgently, he saw red, forgot any emotional ties he had for the Ghost and allowed anger to consume his heart. Once he'd allowed himself to believe the Ghost had gone behind his back and betrayed him, slaughtering all of his best men, right under his nose, there was no going back.

"He called upon the captains around the table with him to gather their best men, together they were going to exact revenge on the mad man and continue with their quest," the Watchman said, looking to Billy and asking if he could have another cigarette by rubbing his thumb and forefinger together.

He took his time rolling as a he contemplated how best to tell what happened next.

"What happened to the Ghost?" Jake prompted, worried the Watchman had lost his train of thought he'd fallen silent for so long.

The Watchman lit his cigarette, looked at Jake, and decided to proceed.

"When the captain marched above deck, leaving Captain Jones and the others below, it was raining. The wind had picked up too. We looked across in the direction of the Liberty Pioneer and even in those few moments the rain, and the wind grew tenfold—I'd never seen a storm like it," he said, a touch of fear creeping into his voice.

"Water flew through the air all around us, hard. The lightning was blinding, the thunder deafening—it was like the storm was on top of us, or we were inside it.

"Some of the men thought it was the Ghost's doing, and nearly fled back below deck.

"But no man, not even the Ghost, was capable of this," the Watchman said gravely, his voice again fearful. He took another swig of rum, and then another.

Issy thought he looked like someone in therapy, trying to get years of torment they'd been bottling up off their chest.

"I was about to go to the captain's side to ask him what he wanted to do. The storm was unreal, and I knew if we stayed on deck and marvelled at it any longer, it would sweep us clean off and into the sea.

"But before I could move everything just—slowed down. Except, *we* didn't. The noise from the lightning, the crashing waves, the wind ripping through the sails and across the sea, all of it just

141

stopped, and everything fell silent. But we could still see individual drops of rain, still touch them, still feel them, and yet we were no longer affected by them too. Our hair was still and no longer troubled by the wind, the water stayed just away so we no longer had to squint our eyes to see." He paused, checking their reactions, his eyes daring them to disagree. But no one said a word.

The Watchman took a breath and tried to calm himself.

"Then we heard voices—we all did. At first it was just this *noise*," he said, screwing up his face as he remembered. "Then the voices separated."

"It… they… had been speaking together, at once, but then there was just one… the sea."

"I'm sorry, what? You're telling us the sea was talking to you now?" Billy blurted out, his voice dripping thick with cynicism.

The Watchman twitched and almost reached for his dagger. He'd never let anyone talk to him like that, not even the captain. He caught himself just in time, remembering his objective.

"Her voice was bitter, loud, and angry" he continued, this time no one, especially not Billy, dared to make a sound. "Like the crashing of the waves or the rushing of a waterfall. She spoke of when the Caribbean seas had been full of nothing but life, and beauty, and then men had come, and now death accompanied the other creatures of the deep.

"I could sense them, the fish, and the other creatures, as she spoke to the captain… I could feel the threat. She told us they were Caribbean gods. Her voice slowed and the water that had been keeping its distance in the air around us slowly settled on our skin, growing in volume instead of dripping away. It felt like we were going to be drowned where we stood.

"When she finished, the water covering our bodies dropped to our feet and we gasped for breath. We heard the air and the land, telling us they were the protectors, and the keepers… and they told us they'd been following us.

"They said that for eternity their territory had remained an undisturbed paradise in the world. The seas, the islands, and the skies that were theirs to guard and nurture, had remained unharmed and had thrived under their watchful eyes, a hidden utopia on earth.

"But then the first ships had arrived, and more had followed behind them. And then more, and more.

"Fighting, bloodshed, and death. That's all they said the ships and the men aboard brought with them.

"They said they had seen into the future, and had seen men taking over their islands, their seas, and their skies. Burning, and polluting, scarring, and destroying everything that was theirs to protect.

"When they listened to the captain's ambition to form a new paradise, ordered and secret, and leaving all other men behind, they had sensed an opportunity," the Watchman said, lifting the bottle of rum high to get a good mouthful of what remained.

Issy, Jake, and Billy sat, barely moving, partly through fear—the Watchman's wild eyes had not returned to normal since Billy's interruption—but also through fascination. Whether it was their strange surroundings, the silence only broken by the living jungle noises, or the fact they were all deliriously exhausted and still in shock from the attack earlier they didn't know, but his story about Caribbean gods and the creatures of the sea wasn't sounding as far-fetched to them as it should have.

"They told the captain they were willing to give him everything he'd ever wanted, and more." The Watchman laughed slightly.

"They told us there were a handful of the most beautiful islands in the Caribbean, completely unknown to man, and that they would guide us safely to where we could start our new land—and that we could live there undisturbed for eternity.

"They promised that while our futures were aligned, ours and theirs, they would support us where and when they saw fit. They said they were the storms, the rain, the wind, the thunder, and all the creatures above and below the water, and they would appear at our side and help us achieve our ends.

"And they promised the captain one more thing too," the Watchman said. "The very worst imaginable revenge on the Ghost."

"What's the catch?" Jake asked, thinking aloud then panicking at interrupting the Watchman a second time. He flinched but the Watchman just smiled a crooked smile.

"They promised the captain paradise and revenge would be his… providing we met their conditions," he said, staring at Jake.

"First, our lives were our own to take care of. We would need to eat, rest, and heal like we always had, but providing we looked after ourselves we would keep living. If we were careless, or lost in battle, we were on our own and we would still die.

"Second, we could recruit people into our new colony from outside of the islands… but once they'd set foot on the islands, they could never leave.

"Third, our secret must, at all costs, remain hidden. They made it very clear if anyone uncovered the secret location of the islands, the agreement would be broken… and there would be terrible consequences."

"What consequences?" Jake asked quietly.

"War," replied the Watchman. "They said they would go to war with us, and all people in the Caribbean. They said they'd wipe us out."

"Why don't they just do that now? Get rid of everyone and be done with it?" Billy said, speaking for the first time since he'd almost provoked the Watchman to come at him, and being careful to measure his tone correctly not to risk that happening again.

"We've never asked, as that's not a concept I'd like to put in their minds, but there are some theories… I believe it wouldn't be easy for them. We sensed it took great effort for them to slow time and show themselves to us on that night.

"To command the sea, the air, the land, and an entire army of creatures, above and below the water, for long enough to wipe us all out, would require a tremendous and sustained burst of power. As far as we know they've never had to do that before, and perhaps they're wondering if they could do it, just as we are. If they could just wipe us out, I think they would… but I think they need us.

"I have seen what they *can* do though, and I really don't want to be on the receiving end," the Watchman stated.

"Was that all of the conditions? Once your body dies you die, keep the islands a secret from the outside world, and you can bring people to join the colony, but they can't leave?" Issy asked.

"Yes, but there was a clause. They'd seen the bloodbath aboard the Liberty Pioneer, and they'd seen a chance to manipulate things in order to keep us in check, to give us added incentive to guard their islands for them and keep them a secret.

"They used the captain's revenge as a way to bait him into closing the deal. They thought of a revenge so perfect, and so cruel, that no revenge he could have thought of would ever come close.

"Having followed the captain for some time they relied upon his fury, fully expecting him to jump at the chance to save face and inflict misery on his betrayer. The gods took a gamble on us, on the captain, and they won," he said, looking towards the hammock once more.

The effects from the rum were beginning to show and the Watchman's looks in Amy's direction were getting careless. Issy, who hadn't touched a drop not trusting where the drink had come from, caught him staring and bristled, unsure of his intentions and priming herself to spring into action if needed.

"What did they do to the Ghost?" Billy asked.

"They told the captain one of their hidden islands, the most beautiful islands on earth that they'd been protecting for hundreds of years, would be a prison for the Ghost and his crew. The gods would take away time, for him and every one of his men, making it so they were unable to move or leave, living but not living, imprisoned and forced to live in the captain's paradise, but unable to enjoy even a sliver of it, forever.

"The Ghost would be frozen, within sight of the shore and the beautiful emerald sea, but unable to touch it or get even one centimetre (one inch) closer. He would be forced to live, endlessly, while the rest of the world forgot him, carrying on around him as though he wasn't even there," the Watchman's voice grew quiet as the enormity, and the horror, of the Ghost's sentence truly dawned on him.

"As they expected the captain, full of prideful rage and desperate for revenge saw no down side to this. He told the gods yes without even consulting us, yes to all of it. He let ambition and anger rule.

"We heard laughter, *she* was laughing, and while the captain paid no attention I knew she was laughing at us and that the captain had made a momentous mistake," the Watchman said, hanging his head close to his chest, his wild, dark hair swaying freely in front of him.

"But... he got everything he wanted?" Jake asked, still not understanding.

"Yes, he did, but at a cost. The gods had used the situation with the Ghost for security. They knew humans were fallible and prone to temptation, and they knew that given a set of rules without any visible reminder of what would happen if the rules weren't kept, men and women were almost certain to break them, either through neglect or malice, one way or another they wouldn't be upheld.

"By caging the Ghost on the island right in the middle of our supposed new paradise they were placing a physical reminder, and threat, in front of everyone. They'd caged a monster in our midst, one that would be released if they didn't obey.

"The Ghost was the one earthly thing that everyone on the expedition was afraid of... and they were afraid of him before he was locked up. The gods knew that with nothing else to do but plot his own revenge inside his head, the longer the Ghost was imprisoned, the more dangerous he became, and the stronger the deterrent.

"In one accord they'd gained the most skilled, and now highly motivated, army to guard and keep secret their most prized islands in the Caribbean, hidden safely from man, forever," he said, lifting the now empty bottle of rum and, seeing it was empty, reaching for the gin.

"They hadn't given the captain everything he'd wanted… they'd taken everything *they* wanted."

CHAPTER 28: THE ESCAPEE

For a few moments no one said a word. The Watchman's thoughts remained with that night on the Red Privateer, and Jake, Issy, and Billy tried to process what they were hearing, not knowing what to make of the brooding man sitting before them who suddenly looked very, very old in the firelight.

"Did you find the islands?" Jake asked finally, remembering again what had brought them there in the first place.

The Watchman looked up at Jake, sensing a chance to make an ally. "Yes, we found them. There are eight of them, hidden deep in the Caribbean Sea. They're like nothing you've ever seen," the Watchman said, his eyes gleaming.

"They're shrouded in a thick layer of mist, so thick it felt like we were never going to come out the other side. When we did finally break through, the islands rose out of the water like living things, huge, breathing monsters resting next to each other, with only a fraction breaking the water's surface and the rest of their secrets below the waves.

"Each island is so wild and overgrown with thick jungle, and…" the Watchman stopped himself.

Even though he knew telling them about the islands wouldn't break the treaty and send the Caribbean gods to war with the world, he still felt uneasy.

"We weren't the only inhabitants," he said, almost in a whisper.

"What do you mean?" Jake asked, leaning in and desperate for the Watchman to continue.

"There are *things* that live there. Creatures that don't exist outside of the islands, I can't say more than that but some of the men believe that if the gods do turn on us… unleashing them will be the first thing they do."

Jake badly wanted to know more but, not wanting to rile the Watchman as Billy had done, he forced himself to bite his tongue.

"We thought we were free but really they'd enslaved us, forced us to be their protectors from our own kind," the Watchman said. "Plundering ships changed from a hunt for treasures, to a chore.

"We had lookouts positioned all over and if one of them sighted a potential threat they'd trigger an alarm, and ships would be detailed to take care of the threat.

"The gods stayed true to their side of the bargain and always helped us. If they saw we needed cover they'd send storm clouds; if we needed extra muscle, lightning would fly from the sky and set entire ships ablaze… or the sharks would arrive," the Watchman added.

Jake, Issy, and Billy froze. "Sharks?" Jake repeated, his heart sinking.

"Sometimes I'd hear *her* as they got closer, sometimes not. The lightning was preferable to be honest, more merciful. When the sea god turned up in the form of those hideous fish… well she likes to make it messy. I've seen her attack whole ships, sometimes in a frenzy and sometimes as one giant monster. Men who fall or flee overboard don't have a chance. I've even seen one land on deck and rip a man in half.

"The captain made it his mission to tie up all loose ends after every capture, especially after what happened with the runaway. The sharks often cleaned up after him and made sure no one was left to speak," he said.

Billy was grateful for the fading fire and the blackness outside. He felt sick and could feel the colour draining from his face. The thought that the monster he'd encountered could have been the same thing the Watchman was describing really disturbed him, and, if it was true, it confirmed a suspicion he still had nightmares about—it hadn't attacked out of instinct, it had *wanted* to murder them.

"In the beginning, the captain really believed we were keeping the islands a secret for ourselves, to build the kind of countries that would elevate mankind. But it didn't pan out that way, we had the same problems as anywhere else… crime, disease, disorder, death.

"After a while it became obvious we were keeping the islands a secret for them because we were afraid of what would happen if we didn't. We were afraid of them first and foremost, but their backup plan had worked too, there was constant fear of the island prison and what would happen if the Ghost and his men got free… especially after Michael escaped."

"Someone escaped?" Issy asked stunned. "How?"

"The gods had instructed us to transport the Ghost and his men to the smallest island in the middle of the others. They said that once we'd positioned them there they would make sure they never left, or moved, providing no one discovered them.

"The captain kept them bound, gagged, and blindfolded from the moment we set sail until the moment we arrived at our destination. The Ghost, nor any of his men, saw daylight again until we were there; they weren't permitted food, and only rationed a little water to make sure they survived the voyage, even though some of them perished along the way.

"When we anchored, the captain ordered us to collect them from below deck and dump them on the sand. We removed their blindfolds and the captain looked each of them in the eye, before heading further inland to find their final resting place.

"He found a clearing through the trees, and personally positioned the Ghost so he had a good view of the water. I saw him say something close to his ear then he walked away and didn't look back, leaving the gods to do the rest.

"We stayed moored just off shore for a few days, the captain wanting to make sure they really were trapped, and to revel in their misery. He sent a small boat back to check on them and even went once himself at the end of the third day. Whatever he saw must have convinced him because he returned serious-faced and ordered we set sail and set about forming our new utopia immediately.

"He was extremely lax in creating a parameter. I think what he'd seen had shocked him, and he'd assumed there was no way the Ghost or any of his men were ever going anywhere, so when he did finally task various men and vessels to guard the area, tracking any movement in or out… it was too late," the Watchman said.

"What do you mean too late?" Billy asked.

"Someone got out," replied the Watchman.

"Within the fleet we had certain vessels just for supplies, containing everything from food and drink to weapons. Around a month after we'd arrived on the islands the captain had asked some of the men to do a stocktake, and they duly reported one of the rum boats was missing.

"The captain knew he'd left a window open and a smaller boat could easily have slipped the handful of warships that he'd set up, there were still plenty of gaps.

"He was furious and blamed anyone else that he could. He returned to the island where the Ghost and his men were held prisoner, to inspect them close up again and make sure they really were still frozen, and to try to ascertain who was missing.

"I didn't know Michael well. He wasn't a part of the Ghost's inner circle, which perhaps explained how he managed to get away without anyone realising. Our best guess was that, somehow, he'd avoided being thrown in the makeshift cage at the bottom of the ship ready to be transported, but he'd still boarded, unable to escape straight away and with nowhere else to go. He then probably stowed away somewhere aboard the prisoner ship, not able to reach and free his crew, and was trapped as soon as we were out on open water.

"We think he must have watched on helplessly as his shipmates were unloaded on to the island.

"Choosing the rum boat was a smart move. With all of the Ghost's men thought to be frozen no one was really on their guard, and it must have been relatively easy for him to pick his moment and sail to safety as soon as he had a clear run," the Watchman said with an element of admiration.

"The captain went out of his mind trying to hunt him down. He sent watchmen like me on to almost every conceivable port island in the Caribbean to cut him off, but it was too late.

"There was one sighting in the Cayman Islands, but the intel was days old and Michael was long gone by then.

"At first we'd assumed he'd made his escape as soon as he'd had the chance, but the timing of the sighting suggested something more cunning. He'd disappeared just days after the captain had set up his treasury on the island most detached, and furthest to the north.

"The gods only gave the location of their islands to Captain Sands, and shortly after we arrived he divvied them up, allocating five to the five fleet captains, one for himself and his most trusted men, the smallest island in the middle was for the Ghost, and he held one back for his treasury. He'd done his best to keep it a secret, taking only a skeleton crew, and even blindfolding them until they were right on top of their destination. But after the rum boat had been found missing, the captain searched his own ship too and found evidence of a stowaway.

"He's convinced to this day Michael was on board and knows where his secret island is. He's stockpiled all of the gold, jewels, money, supplies, some weapons, and anything that he deems of greatest value there. By the time Michael escaped it was too late to change the treasury's location because the other men already knew where the rest of the islands were. Instead, he had the men construct a huge building with a series of vaults, and stuck armed guards on every entrance. He even had to build lodgings for them to sleep, blindfolding both the new guards arriving and those departing the island whenever there was a change in shift. Only men would build a bank in paradise, and only Sands would build one like that," he added, shaking his head.

Jake, Issy, and Billy tried to picture the mysterious northern island with what must be the richest bank in the world, full of stolen loot, gathered, and stockpiled over hundreds of years, and protected by guards who didn't even know where they were in order to keep its location hidden—and they wondered if the bottle maps they were carrying would reveal it to them.

"Knowing that someone was out there who could return and break the treaty, steal everything he had, and set the Ghost free drove the captain insane," continued the Watchman. "He worried constantly that his life's work would be scuppered owing to his one mistake.

"Captain Sands became more like a prison guard awaiting an uprising than the leader of men he'd wanted so badly to be. He even changed the name of our ship from the Liberty Pioneer, to the Devil's Liberty in a swipe at the Caribbean gods and the lifetime of servitude they'd tricked him in to, although I'm pretty sure they weren't bothered by that." The Watchman snorted.

"And all the while the Ghost's legend grew and grew. Even the newborns brought up on the islands were told the stories. They were taught never get too close to his island prison, and why it was so important to keep their world a secret from outsiders. Despite being unable to move, the Ghost's power and influence radiated, and only became stronger the more his stories were recounted... you can imagine how that went down with the captain.

"The Ghost had become a legend, while the man who'd started the legend rotted and faded from existence, unable to live or die. Worst of all... I don't think he even did it," the Watchman said ever so slightly louder, laying the first piece of information he genuinely hoped Amy was listening to.

"What do you mean?" asked Jake quickly.

"The night the captain agreed to the treaty and the deal was done he immediately gathered as many men together as he could to retake the Liberty Pioneer, and I was one of them.

"When we boarded the ship expecting to find the Ghost and his crew ready to fight to the death, we found no such thing. Bodies lay where they fell across the deck, and there was blood everywhere, but the ship was eerily quiet.

"We proceeded to search for the Ghost, and found him with his most trusted soldiers, relaxing, and drinking in the captain's quarters.

"The captain's first reaction was to assume the Ghost meant to insult him further, by first slaying his crew then celebrating his victory sitting at the captain's table. He wanted to cut them all down there and then, and the promise of the far crueller revenge the gods had promised was the only thing that kept him from doing so.

"But that's not to say they were completely unharmed. During the beating that followed only one of his men said a word, the rest remained defiantly silent, including the Ghost. The captain, of course, took this as an admission of guilt, which I think was the final insult for one of the Ghost's men, an older sailor who'd been with the Ghost a long time. He couldn't keep quiet. Whenever he had a chance to take air in between punches he raved about how the Ghost had saved all of them.

"He said the captain's crew had been planning a mutiny, that they were going to sneak over to the Red Privateer and take advantage of all the leaders being off-guard in one room, at the same time. They were going to slaughter everyone and take control with Captain Jones taking charge of the whole fleet once everyone else, the Ghost, Sands and all their men, were out of the way.

"No one else said a word to confirm or deny his claims, and I'm not even sure anyone else really listened, they were so riled up by the captain's need for revenge.

"But I think he was telling the truth, that somehow the Ghost had overheard of a plot to take down the leaders of the expedition, including the captain, in one hit, and in order to prevent the attack and to stamp out the threat he took out the conspirators and everyone they may have conspired with.

"I believe he then sat down with his men satisfied with a job well done and planned to greet the captain on his return before he boarded to tell him what had happened. Only Lewis got away and brought them running earlier than expected."

"Imagine that, locked away inside your own head, wrongly imprisoned," Amy's voice interrupted the Watchman and made everyone jump. She was standing next to the hammock; none of them had heard her get up.

"How are you feeling?" Issy asked, going over to her friend, cautiously. Unable to tell how much of herself she was, she decided to give her a hug before bringing her over to share the crate she'd been sitting on.

"That's some story," said Billy, sitting back on his crate and stretching out his big legs one at a time. He hadn't meant to, but his scepticism came out in his voice again and he almost fell backwards with fear as he caught the Watchman's glare.

"And it still doesn't explain why you are no longer with them, and suddenly on our side... I'm assuming you're now on our side?" Amy said calmly, cocking her head slightly.

Billy, Jake, and Issy looked at each other and felt their hearts beat faster.

The Watchman returned Amy's stare carefully, trying to work out how much of the Ghost was in there.

With Amy now awake he realised he'd missed his chance to find out how she'd become like this, but he did sense another opportunity.

"Captain Sands has lost control," he began strongly, knowing he could never go back to the Devil's Liberty so there was no point hedging his bets at this point.

"I don't know if it's paranoia, or his fears are justified, but he's convinced someone is coming to steal his throne. His rule has turned to chaos, and the only way he can keep his fleet from abandoning him is through fear. I should have left sooner but I didn't see any other option," the Watchman continued.

"What changed?" Jake asked.

"The powers are shifting. The gods are at odds with each other and not all of them support his reign anymore.

"I had an opportunity to escape, and I took it. I wanted to run, as far away from him, the Devil's Liberty, these islands, and the Caribbean Sea as I could possibly get. But I realised no matter how far I run he will never stop coming after me. I've escaped from one lifetime of fear for another, where I'll constantly be looking over my shoulder.

"There is only one option for me. I have to fight," he said truthfully.

He'd been as honest as he could be without revealing either his desperation, or the reason for his expulsion from the ship in the first place. He looked at Amy and couldn't read her eyes, or the Ghost's.

"But why help *us?*" Billy said, still not sold.

"They're hunting you, and I knew the captain would send more men. Whatever you're doing here has the captain scared, which makes it worth protecting," he said.

Amy wasn't convinced and was about to press him further when the Watchman stood up.

"It's late," he said. "Get some rest and I can guide you to the cliff top at first light." Then he walked out in to the jungle.

He kept walking for a few minutes until he was sure he had some privacy, found a clearing, and pulled a half-smoked cigar from his jacket pocket. Using the petrol-lighter, he brought it to life in his lips and puffed away until his head was hidden by a cloud of thick smoke.

I need to make sure.

Before the Watchman could decide whether to commit his allegiance, and set the Ghost free, he needed to know how the Ghost was likely to react. Somehow, he had to get the Ghost to promise not to kill him, through Amy.

If the Ghost was to be unleashed after so many years of torment, the Watchman needed to be damn sure he was either on his side, or far, far away and out of the firing line.

CHAPTER 29: CLOSER

A bright light flickered over the top of the darkness in front of him that hadn't been there before. Faint at first, it had grown stronger and more vivid the longer he'd stared at it, willing it so. As it had grown, so had the scene around the light, becoming more visible as the vision brightened.

What are you up to?

The Ghost concentrated hard on the moving image, straining his focus to identify those within it. He recognised the blonde-haired woman with the two men and had seen them enough to know them well now. At first he had dismissed them out of hand, unable to understand how he held such a strong connection with someone so close to such inconsequential people.

But he had been surprised, and seen a resilience and resourcefulness he hadn't expected, especially when Sands' men had attacked on the plateau. His connection had been at its strongest then, and he enjoyed the confrontation. A taste of things to come—if he could just guide them to him.

He scolded himself for underestimating them, something he never thought he would do. Men had constantly underestimated him when he was growing up, mostly his father, until the Ghost had saved his life when he was only ten.

His mother had passed away some years earlier and it had been only him and his father at home, alone in their big farm house in the countryside. The Ghost, still Thomas Brown back then, had jumped from his bed hearing someone break in. He crept to his father's room, to find him being savagely beaten by a much bigger man. He could see straight away he was size-wise no match for the intruder, and even at ten years old he knew if he ran into the room he might become another victim.

Instead, Thomas had calmly thought about how he could get the upper hand. He anticipated the man would eventually return downstairs to search the rest of the house, and it gave him an idea. He ran to the kitchen and took the biggest knife he could find from the drawer, then went back upstairs and slid behind a large bookshelf on the landing, wedging himself in the narrow gap so he could just see out.

He listened and watched as the man left his father's room and started in the direction of Thomas's bedroom. Unable to find Thomas the man returned to the landing and Thomas pounced, pushing him as hard as he could so he would fall down the stairs.

Thomas stood at the top watching with satisfaction as the man cracked his head once, then twice more on his way down, landing with his arms and legs splayed unnaturally and his head unmoving. Wanting to make sure, Thomas tore down the stairs after him and plunged the knife into his chest repeatedly, blood spraying onto his white nightshirt.

Certain the intruder was dead, and alone, Thomas returned upstairs and, covered in blood, crept into his father's room to see if he was still breathing. He was, but barely.

Thomas never found out what happened to the body, his father had said he had taken care of it. All he knew was that the police never came, and his father had treated him with a lot more respect after that.

The Ghost looked harder next to the fire—someone else was with them. He strained his mind to make the vision clearer and managed to give the scene a degree more clarity.

Daniel.

He'd seen the Watchman step out of the shadows and assassinate Tobias on the ledge, but he thought he had disappeared back into the darkness and hadn't seen him since.

The Ghost had puzzled over the Watchman's contribution to the fight. He knew Daniel as one of the captain's men from old, always by his side.

One of the captain's men, attacking the captain's men.

He tuned back into his vision and heard Daniel's voice. He was talking... *about him.*

He hadn't heard a lot, but the words he had caught made him strain harder.

He knows I'm innocent.

As he listened he went over that night again, remembering the fear and derision on the faces of those who had condemned him. They all had been so eager to rid themselves of him, a man they called a monster, despite all they had gained.

He remembered Edmund tell their accusers what had really happened. He knew no one would believe them and was angry Edmund had said anything at all. It was too late. They'd been sloppy, allowing Lewis to escape, and now they were paying the price. If they'd gotten to the captain first he would have believed them, but him finding them, in his quarters, looking like they were celebrating their kill. No, no one was going to think of them as anything other than traitors.

But the Ghost had been wrong. Daniel had heard, and he'd believed them to be innocent.

The Ghost tried to process what it meant, his elation turning into fury almost instantly. He screamed uncontrollably inside his head.

You knew... and yet you did nothing.

The Ghost studied Daniel closely until he could no longer see his form in the darkness, and the entire vision faded away leaving him with nothing but the familiar treeline and gentle unreachable waves lapping at the shore in the distance.

CHAPTER 30: FAILURE

Leonard stood in front of Captain Sands' desk feeling particularly pleased with himself.

After he'd half jumped half fallen off the ledge, he'd landed in a heap in some dry bushes. His landing had been painful, and he was covered in bruises, but nothing was broken and most importantly—he was alive.

At first he hadn't known what to do. He had never been in a position to make decisions for himself before.

After laying still for some time he'd heard the noises from above fade away and then stop altogether. He assumed it was safe to move as Daniel, the wild woman, and her friends must have moved on.

It had taken him hours to scramble and slide down the muddy slope. He collided with rocks and sharp branches so many times he felt like giving up, but the thought of being back on board the Devil's Liberty, and then home to his well-stocked pantry and comfortable bed had kept him going.

Eventually he had made it to a point where he could fall no more and assumed he must be near the beach. Excitement welled in his chest and he lumbered forward, his pace increasing as much as his giant battered body would allow.

It had taken him a lot longer than anticipated to find the row boat they had come over in, but failing light and fatigue were against him, and he just couldn't remember where it had been left.

Exhausted and frustrated he had sat on his arse and sunk deep into the sand, wrapping his huge arms around his knees, unable to think of what he should do next—which was when he spotted it, over to his right, poking out from between two coconut trees just where they had left it.

Leonard lurched to his feet as quickly as he could pushing the pain from his heavy limbs out of his mind as much as he could.

He remembered the Devil's Liberty had not anchored far away, and he could see a particularly dark patch of clouds that looked familiar.

Pushing the boat out on to the waves he managed to flop inside like an enormous barracuda. Grasping hold of the oars he steered himself to where he thought his ship was hidden.

He arrived just before nightfall. The men hauled him aboard and sent him straight to the captain who they said was in a foul mood. They warned him to be careful, but Leonard only knew the captain to be ill-tempered these days and paid them little attention.

Standing before Captain Sands, having relayed the battle of the plateau with as much gusto as he could considering he still hadn't eaten anything, he was trying to read the expression on his captain's face in the gloom of the cabin.

He didn't look pleased. Leonard waited patiently to be dismissed so he could head to the kitchen to fill his belly that was painfully empty and kept making loud awkward grumbling noises.

"He's alive," the captain spat out the words.

Leonard wasn't sure what to say. He felt like there had been a question, but he'd missed it and had no idea what the answer was.

Still standing, his belly growling louder by the minute, temptation was building in Leonard to just turn and leave.

Surely, if he wanted something more from me he would have said by now?

He waited another minute then his painful hunger won out. Leonard turned and, without a word, made for the door of Captain Sands' cabin.

His hand had just made it to the handle when he felt a sharp pain in his side, starting at his hip and moving all the way up underneath his right armpit.

Instinctively Leonard reached with his left arm to feel what was causing the pain. But all he could feel was a hot wet patch.

162

Confused, he wondered if somehow he had rubbed up against something on his travels and just hadn't noticed.

His thought was interrupted abruptly as the captain pushed him hard in the back. Leonard tried to put his hands out to stop himself, but he suddenly felt weak, and was unable to prevent his temple smacking first the door, and then the ground.

Captain Sands kicked Leonard's head out of the way with his heavy boots so he could open the door, then stepped over his body as Leonard bled out underneath him. The captain grabbed an arm in each of his and dragged the deadening weight to the side of the ship.

Lightning crackled overhead making the wet trail of blood Leonard left behind him shine brightly on the ship's deck.

Another bolt flashed overhead, catching one of the sails nearest to Sands' head and catching fire.

He took his dagger from his belt and drove it hard into the back of Leonard's skull, before heaving his huge corpse into the choppy water.

He watched in silence, unperturbed by the wind and the rain that seemed to be doing its best to irritate him. One by one the sharks appeared, taking small chunks here and there, colouring the sea red, before one hideous creature erupted from directly underneath Leonard and bit him clean in two.

Satisfied this time no one would be coming back to haunt him, the captain looked at the sky as though he had laid down an unspoken challenge.

In response, another bolt of lightning destroyed one of the masts, obliterating it to burning ash in front of him, but still Sands did not move.

"I suggest you start helping me again," he spat, still looking up at the sky.

The rain continued to fall, and the captain's men still on deck exchanged glances. Some looked confused and some afraid, but all knew it was best for them to mind their own business.

Satisfied his words had been heard the captain marched back to his cabin.

"If you want war, I'll give you a war. I'll burn these islands to dust before I hand them over to you or that traitor," he said, stepping through Leonard's still warm blood.

CHAPTER 31: FINAL ASCENT

Jake listened to the crackle of rain as it made its way through the maze of leaves, before finding the ever-muddier trail at his feet.

Unable to sleep they had decided to gather their things and ready themselves to set off a bit before dawn, making the most of the cooler, fresher air.

The Watchman had heard them rummaging around through the thin canvas dividing their rooms and worried they had decided to leave him behind.

Not sure whether they were just up early, or were trying to escape without him, and failing badly, he waited until it sounded like they had finished their work, then stood in front of their side of the tent, ready to go.

He hadn't made a sound and when Issy, who was closest to the opening on their side, had rolled up the flap of canvas and found the Watchman's dark shadow looming in the space between herself and the jungle, it had taken all her concentration to stop herself screaming and alerting half the island to their whereabouts.

Instead, she'd bit her lip, nodded at the Watchman who returned her acknowledgement, before alerting the others they had company, as subtly as she possibly could.

They hadn't intended to leave the Watchman behind, but equally they hadn't planned to make any great effort to wake him if he happened to still be sleeping when they set off. He had saved Jake's life, and through him they had gathered more intel on the opposition they faced in a few hours, than they had managed to piece together in an entire week, they also knew he would prove extremely handy in a fight, assuming he kept on their side.

But despite all that, he had hunted them down in an attempt to kill them in Barbados, none of them trusted him and Billy thought he was completely delusional.

"He gives me the creeps," Issy whispered to Billy, after the two of them had allowed an extra half a metre (almost two feet) between them and Amy up ahead, with Jake and the Watchman in front of her. Issy kept her eyes on Amy as she spoke and made sure they didn't fall back too far in case she needed to help her friend.

"I know, me too. Looks like we're stuck with him for now," agreed Billy. "He said we've rattled the captain. It *must* be to do with the maps. Somehow the captain knows we have a way of finding his secret island with his giant bank. Maybe that's all this guy's after too," he said, nodding towards the Watchman up ahead.

"You think he's just using us to find the next anchor, so he can rob the island?" Issy asked.

"Maybe. I mean it seems most likely to me. He saved Jake to get us on his side, find out what we have, and then he plans to take it from us when he gets the chance," Billy said. "And I'm not convinced about the whole, 'We're three-hundred-year-old pirate demigods' speech either," he added, quietly.

"Yeh. I'm trying not to dwell on that, this is all pretty surreal," Issy said, looking around her nervously.

"What if the maps lead to the Ghost?" she added, worrying. It had been the first thing they'd discussed as soon as they were alone.

In hushed whispers Jake, Billy, and Issy had agreed there was a possibility the maps had been left by the runaway to free his crew, but given what the Watchman had told them about the timing of his escape they agreed it was more likely he had left a trail to the money, and they were unanimous they had to carry on and find out regardless—they had come too far not to. Aside from that, they had all been highly sceptical about the Ghost, and the gods of the Caribbean full stop. Amy had remained quiet throughout.

"I think he made all that up, the Ghost, and the wrath of the gods, all of it, to scare us off. Maybe he thinks it'll make it easier to part us with whatever we find," Billy said. "Either way, we need to keep a close eye on this guy and be ready to run."

They decided to tell Jake and Amy the plan at the first available opportunity. They had to be subtle, if the Watchman knew they were a flight risk he might strike first.

Up ahead, Jake kept his eyes on the tree-tops to his left and further out to sea as the rain clouds overhead lightened slightly as dawn broke, casting an eerie hue over everything.

Not concentrating on his footsteps he slipped suddenly, his right shoe sliding in the river of mud below him, causing him to topple forward. He stopped himself with both arms outstretched, burying his hands in cascading mud up to his wrists.

The Watchman turned to find out what had caused the disturbance. Unused to trekking in a group, with inexperienced and less skilled companions, it was easy to make out his frustration, even at first light and in the continuing rain.

Jake quickly scrabbled back to his feet, Amy and Billy helping him.

The Watchman slowed the pace a fraction, but still kept them marching on. The others tried to keep up as best they could, struggling against the tide of growing mud at their feet, increasing in intensity as the slope steepened and the rain continued to fall.

Finally, the trail rounded its last bend to reveal a wide flat expanse of shrubland ahead, and a ripple of excitement passed through the chain of hikers as they sensed the finish line.

Jake, Amy, Billy, and Issy had kept watch for a suitable route to flee whenever they could, but the concentration required to navigate the last section of the trail, at the rate the Watchman had wanted them to go, had made escape impossible.

Now they were so close to what they'd come to Antigua to find, thoughts of running anywhere but up to the flat shrubland ahead vanished temporarily from their minds.

Soaked through and covered in mud Jake was the first of their group to make it to the summit, just behind the Watchman. As he staggered around in circles trying to catch his breath and take in the view from all angles, he was dumfounded. He'd never seen nature so breathtakingly beautiful before in his entire life.

From the summit they could see clearly above the tree-tops on all sides, and as he stood staring wide-eyed out to sea, the first morning sunlight fully broke free from the dark clouds, causing the multi-tonal blues and greens to light up and glisten across the bay just below him.

Small islands lay a little further out, and he could even spot a few modern yachts and bright white sailing boats dotted close to the shore.

The view was so spectacular he completely forgot what he was doing there.

"Jake, come look at this!" Billy shouted.

He turned around to see Amy striding towards a wooden shack overlooking rolling green hills covered in lush rainforest inland. She identified the shack as the place most likely to contain the next clue as soon as they had reached the top.

Billy held back for Jake, who eventually left his view, a little reluctantly, to re-join the others, spaced out around the wooden building, searching for the easiest way in.

The shack was the only construction on top of the cliff as far as they could see, and Jake couldn't make out any other obvious, or even less obvious places that they could search. If the anchor wasn't in there, he wasn't sure what they would do next.

"This has to be it," he mumbled to himself, excitement growing inside him.

Amy, becoming agitated, was rattling the door handle in frustration, and it was becoming apparent she was losing herself again, which only heightened Jake's feeling they were in the right place.

The main door was locked and seeing no other obvious entrance Amy grabbed hold of the handle and slammed her shoulder into the wooden panelling, her frustration boiling over. The door splintered and caved, swinging inwards with Amy still attached. Issy, Billy, and Jake bundled in after her.

The Watchman held back and stood in the doorway, blocking out most of the light and also their exit, whether intentionally or unintentionally, Jake wasn't sure.

As he hovered in the entrance the Watchman felt torn. Whether whatever they were looking for led to the treasury, or the Ghost's prison, it didn't matter to him, the deal would still be broken, and the Ghost would be freed. The quicker they found the location, the sooner he'd be out of danger of the Ghost taking control of Amy and trying to beat the coordinates of the islands out of him.

He was pretty certain the only reason the Ghost hadn't done so already was because he didn't have enough control over his host, yet, and was worried if he tried an attack something could go wrong. Amy might get killed, or the Watchman, the only person who actually knew where his prison was, could escape. While the Watchman was helping, or at least not hindering, their quest, their goals were aligned, and it was less risky just to let things play out. If he tried to put the squeeze on the Watchman there was a risk he would clam up for good. The Ghost knew he wouldn't break easily.

But he was also painfully aware that as soon as they had the location of the prison, or the treasury, he became far less valuable to the Ghost. He needed an opportunity to prove his worth, and gain the Ghost's trust, but he was out of time—and that meant he had a pressing decision to make.

He could try and stay with the group and escort them to the islands. He would probably have until they arrived to convince the Ghost not to kill him as soon as he got free, assuming he didn't lose patience and kill him in the form of Amy before they even reached their destination.

Or, he could run, now. He'd be a fugitive from Sands, but he was good at hiding, and arguably Sands, at this point, was the least bad option.

The Watchman twitched nervously as he lingered in the doorway, waiting for a triumphant cry to signal they had found what they were looking for, which he hoped would help him make his mind up.

Inside the shack the others feverishly rummaged for the clue. There was a main room, full of tables and chairs stacked up on top of each other, and a bar at the back, with a doorway behind that led to a kitchen and storage room.

"Looks like no one's been in here for a while," Billy said, inspecting the dust and cobwebs.

Amy quickly scanned the first room and, unable to locate what she'd come for, she slipped behind the bar at the back and renewed her search there.

Jake again looked over to the Watchman standing behind them. He could see he was more animated than usual and looked uneasy. Jake guessed something was wrong, but there was no going back now. If the Watchman tried to rob them, they'd have to fight.

He heard Amy removing boxes from shelves in the back room and throwing them on the ground, the odd bottle smashing loudly, and he went behind the bar to help her—fully aware that she'd be needed if it came down to a brawl.

Within ten minutes the pair of them had opened every box and searched every shelf and cupboard and were still empty-handed. Issy and Billy had done the same in the main room.

Amy screamed in frustration.

"It's not here," Jake said, unable to quite believe they'd come so far, and gone through so much, all for nothing.

The only person not filled with disappointment was the Watchman, who breathed a big sigh of relief.

CHAPTER 32: A NEW PLAN

Issy and Billy looked at Amy, unsure what to say. Both of them suddenly looked up above her head and their eyes widened.

Amy noticed and snapped her head around to see what they were looking at, and even the Watchman took a step inside the shack to get a closer look at the point above Amy's head.

They had been in such a rush when they jammed inside the wooden shack, they hadn't looked up.

Near the ceiling, hanging prominently above the bar, was a pale green anchor. Its colouring perfectly in keeping with the sea-beach theme inside the rest of the shack.

Jake's eyes lit up when he saw it. He was about to say something when Amy let out an animalistic scream of utter frustration.

"What's wrong?" he asked, shocked.

Amy didn't answer she just grabbed one of the chairs that had been neatly stacked on top of the table nearest to her, slammed it down on the ground, and slumped herself down on it.

Then it dawned on him.

"Oh shit," he said quietly.

"What!? What is it?" Issy still didn't know what was going on. She looked to Billy. "Someone tell me what's going on!" she said, frustration laced in her voice.

"If it's up there—it no longer points out there," the Watchman said, waving his arm in the direction of the sea.

Jake cast him a look, suspecting the Watchman had known what they were looking for all along.

"I knew when they were hunting you, when I was hunting you, it was to stop you getting to something. We guessed Michael left a map to the treasury," the Watchman half-lied, feeling all eyes on him.

"When I saw that's what you were looking for," he said, pointing to the anchor floating benignly above the bar. "It wasn't much of a leap to guess it points somewhere." Careful not to dig himself into a hole. "Except, it doesn't."

Jake looked again at the anchor and admitted to himself it did look quite obviously like an arrow.

"We need to find who put it there," the Watchman said, sensing he'd landed his words well and the tide was turning in his favour. As long as they believed they were hunting the treasure they would keep going, and the Watchman would have some time. "This bar's not that old, and most of the people who work around here are based in Bolands, it's less than three miles away."

* * *

Billy was most reluctant, now certain more than ever the Watchman was also after the treasure and planning to double cross them as soon as he had a chance. But they were out of options again, and it would take them forever to find the second clue without him. As long as they kept the first clue hidden and in their possession, the Watchman couldn't just disappear on them. They needed him, and he needed them. What happened when they had both clues he dreaded to think.

"Okay, Bolands," Jake said, shrugging his shoulders slightly and looking at his friends almost apologetically. "We don't have any other leads and hopefully whoever found this anchor is still around, and nearby. We need them to tell us which way the anchor was pointed when they found it."

* * *

The Watchman, satisfied with the plan, went outside.

His objective was still the same, he needed to get closer to the Ghost, and get him onside before he got free. He had to make the Ghost understand his position, why he'd been unable to say or do anything to free him sooner. The Ghost knew what Captain Sands was capable of better than anyone, and the Watchman was confident he'd have little trouble convincing the Ghost he was under duress. More importantly he knew if he could prove himself useful, and an asset, the Ghost would see a purpose for him. He just needed a chance to show his worth.

The Watchman paced up and down on the cliff top, the wind picking up and swirling his dark hair around his shoulders.

And if he thought, after his best efforts, the Ghost would still come after him as soon as the gods' spell was broken, well then he'd need to change his objective significantly.

If that happened he knew he would never be safe and had only one option—he would have to kill Amy, and the Ghost.

CHAPTER 33: BOLANDS

Jake picked at the label of his beer bottle.

He couldn't believe they'd come so far only to hit a complete dead end. When he'd gone through the plan with the others on the cliff top, finding the man or woman who'd found the anchor had sounded like the only logical thing to do. But now, sitting in one bar, surrounded by a dozen random drinkers, he felt hopeless.

"How the hell are we supposed to find them?" he asked, taking a few sips of his beer.

"We'll find them," Issy said instinctively, more to make him feel better than anything else. She put her hand on his arm. Billy noticed and thought about taking Amy's hand or putting his arm around her to try and cheer her up, too. She had barely spoken since they hiked down from the cliff, but he could see she was still not herself and thought better of it.

It had been a hard descent, mainly because of how tired they were. The Watchman had led, taking away the burden of navigating, and yet it had still been a real slog.

When they had arrived, they found somewhere cheap and out of the way to stay. It was run down but clean, with all the rooms on the ground floor, reminding Billy of a roadside motel from back home. Jake and Billy had one room, Amy and Issy another, and the Watchman had his own room.

Utterly spent, they all decided to rest for a bit, trying to sleep, but unable to switch off their minds, fidgeting restlessly in the warm air pushed down from the slow spinning ceiling fans. None of them could relax. They were too hot, there was too much uncertainty, and they didn't feel safe.

They got up early and decided to head to town for breakfast, and begin asking around, as casually as they could to avoid raising suspicion. Too many people knew about the anchors already.

They had told the Watchman they could cover more ground if they split up, and they were relieved he agreed without a fight. He said he was going to get a car and drive along the coast a bit to ask around a few restaurants and bars he knew were particularly popular with islanders more than tourists, saying he could cover everything between Darkwood Beach and Jolly Harbour. The plan was to then meet each other back at a bar in town.

Billy had immediately thought of their bags with the bottles in— there was no way he was leaving them out of his sight.

The four of them had wandered aimlessly around the small town for a bit, not really paying attention to their surroundings or making any real effort to hunt for clues, before deciding to sack off their search for the day and get a drink as soon as the clock struck noon. Deflated and despondent they just needed to get drunk.

"Nice bar, huh?" Billy said, tipping his bottle high to get at the last of the beer. "Four more?"

Jake nodded and Billy leaned closer to the bar to get the barman's attention. They still had a bit of time before the Watchman was due to arrive, and they were enjoying their freedom. It felt good to just be themselves again.

"I don't disagree that he was right about this," Billy said, to pick up a thread of conversation they had started earlier. "I mean we had to pick the trail up again somewhere, right? But how far do we follow this guy?"

"I don't know that we're following him," Jake said a little defensively, worrying the others blamed him for being in Bolands. "It's more that, at the moment, there only seems to be one option, and he knows the island better than we do."

"But if he does find the person who put the anchor in that shack, why would he tell us?" asked Issy, the thought coming to her for the first time.

"Because we know which way the first compass pointed, and without us he doesn't know where the lines would cross," Amy said, finishing her beer as a fresh bottle arrived.

"But he doesn't know that, does he?" Issy said.

"I suspect he does," replied Amy. "Otherwise he'd have to follow the line out in to the sea from wherever it pointed, never sure whether he'd veered slightly off course and missed his mark. He will have guessed there's another anchor and might have guessed that's what we were doing in Barbados when he first found us. He needs us... for now."

"Well, at least we're still in the game," Billy said, determined to enjoy their time without the Watchman. "Cheers to that." He held his bottle up to toast. The others clinked their bottles to his.

For a while they made small talk about nothing more than their surroundings, taking Billy's hint and taking a break from the hunt, out loud at least.

Jake was still keeping a close eye on the skies while they were in the bar. They had been grey since arriving and he couldn't tell if the clouds were getting darker, or if he was just being paranoid. The air was muggy and warm, and no rain was falling, and a light breeze even occasionally made it as far as where they were sat through the open windows. Jake decided to leave it.

"We've got time for one more I think, before he gets here," Billy said. "In?"

Jake nodded. Amy had barely touched her latest bottle and ignored Billy outright and Issy, who was looking a little glassy-eyed, held her hand up as a pass.

"Two more," Billy shouted over to the barman.

When they arrived, he took the bottles passing one to Jake.

"You think it's anyone in here?" he asked, noticing Jake staring at an elderly man with an empty whiskey glass.

"No idea. We can't ask everyone in Antigua,' Jake said, almost laughing.

Billy took a long swig of his beer and placed the bottle back on the bar. He folded his arms, relaxed on his stool, and let his eyes wander, settling on a different drinker and wondering if it was them.

He had just spotted a wiry, unkempt man by the window who he was going to point out to Jake as a potential candidate, when his eyes were drawn to what was outside the window instead.

He turned back to Jake quickly to find his friend was already looking.

"That does not look good," Jake said, getting Amy and Issy's attention too. He hadn't been mistaken; the clouds were getting darker. "What do you think they're planning?"

"I don't know... but there's someone who might," Billy pointed towards the door. The Watchman had just arrived and was looking around the room for them.

Billy raised his bottle slightly higher in the air, and when he saw the Watchman had seen him, he nodded in his direction and put his arm down.

"Maybe let's try and act like we haven't spent the last hour talking about him," Jake hissed, breaking the awkward silence that had descended.

Moments later the Watchman was standing behind Amy, who hadn't even turned to acknowledge him. Jake, Billy, and Issy, turned their heads to face him but none of them were quite sure how to greet him.

"Nothing," he said, getting straight down to business. "I visited every place I could think of, but no one knows anything about the shack on the cliff."

"Yeh, we asked around a bit then settled in here, as you can see we didn't get too far. Beer?" Billy asked, ignoring the anxious looks from Issy and Jake.

To their surprise, the Watchman nodded in acceptance and pulled up a stool.

Billy ordered three more beers, passing one to Jake and one to the Watchman when they arrived.

"We were just discussing what's out there," Billy said, pointing to the open window. The dark clouds looking more ominous by the minute and the wind was picking up too. A strong gust whistled through the bar causing their clothes and hair to flap.

"They're coming," he said, taking a long drink of his beer.

"We gathered that," Amy said, still not looking up. "Any idea on their next move, considering up until very recently... you were one of them."

"The captain won't want any of you to leave the island. He'll probably have amassed a small army by now," the Watchman said.

"And they're coming here? Now?" Issy asked, almost shouting and looking nervously towards the door, expecting dozens of three-hundred-year-old pirates to come screaming through the bar at them.

The Watchman looked to the sky. "They'll make their move soon. I think we have time... but not long."

"Okay. So, what do we do?" Jake asked, standing up and feeling the beers. He was angry with himself for allowing them to waste most of the day, and for just sitting, defeated and waiting, while danger was coming for them. They knew it was a bad idea, but just needed a break so badly they had caved.

"There was one thing," the Watchman said, and all eyes turned on him. "It may be nothing, but one of the men I questioned runs a food hut along the coast. He said he had no idea what I was talking about, but I think he was holding back.

"He was scared. He's part of the resistance and knew who I was. I don't think he found the anchor, but I think he knew of it. He has a brother who works at another bar not far from here," he said.

"And why exactly didn't you mention this when you came in?" Amy snapped, jumping up from her bar stool and turning to face him.

Despite still looking herself on the surface in her short, stone-coloured utility shirt dress, tan ankle boots, and dark red lipstick, even Issy was struggling to find her friend.

The Watchman looked at her carefully. He'd never been more convinced the Ghost was looking back at him and calling the shots.

"I didn't want to report back anything until it was substantiated… but now it seems we are running out of time, and options," he said.

Amy stared at him, simmering once more, the Ghost in her eyes. He was gaining more control over Amy, he could feel it, and the temptation to tear the Watchman to pieces was almost overwhelming.

"Well we better get moving then," Amy said, shoving past the Watchman hard and knocking him into the table behind him.

CHAPTER 34: INVASION

"The boats should all be near their marks now, Captain," said Aaron, the Devil's Liberty's quartermaster.

"A hundred of our best men, split into ten factions, and set to beach in ten different locations around the island. From there they'll make their way inland, searching every settlement. Do you have any further orders?"

Captain Sands stared in the direction of the island in front of them.

"No. Now we wait," he replied, picturing his men wading through the waves of the shallow waters dragging their boats behind them, marching up on to deserted beaches, and slipping silently into the jungle unnoticed.

His mind wandered back to the night he had found the Ghost in his cabin, and his blood boiled. He cursed the gods for tricking him. He should have killed him then and there.

Then he thought of the group who had come looking and grew even more frustrated. Despite his best efforts he still had no idea who they were or how they were connected, but somehow they had completely disturbed the natural order of things, and now had the Watchman helping them.

Anger surged through his body as he thought of the Watchman. After so many years of being vigilant, one drunken night had caused him to be careless—again.

"He'll get his," Sands muttered, calming himself with the thought it wasn't too late to make amends.

When his men found the four outsiders, and the Watchman, their instructions were simple—kill them on sight and bring their bodies to him.

CHAPTER 35: CLOSING IN

According to the Watchman the brother's bar was just outside of town, and he would take them there in the dark grey Mitsubishi pick-up truck parked outside.

He told them he had hired it to get himself quickly around the surrounding bays and beaches, but Issy, Jake, and Billy pretty much assumed he had stolen it, and Amy, no longer cared.

They were all just interested in making progress and escaping Antigua before the captain's men caught up to them.

Jake watched for anything unusual out of the rear window of the truck as the Watchman pushed the vehicle along the dirt roads. Every person he saw looked suspicious to him as paranoia set in. But he told himself to stay calm, the rain hadn't started yet—they still had time.

The Watchman took a sharp left shortly after skidding past a row of houses and entered a long treelined street. Up on the right, Jake could see activity outside one of the buildings, lights, music, and people milling around.

"That'll be it then," he said, hoping the man they were looking for was inside.

The Watchman parked up on the opposite side of the road. Jake could see the place was packed, and a few drinkers at outside tables had already noticed their arrival and were looking over curiously.

Their eyes widened when they saw the big figures of the Watchman and Billy lumber out from the front, and Jake, Issy, and Amy from the back.

Jake was first to spot the stares and looked at himself, then at the others.

The Watchman was wearing his usual loose, open, off-white shirt, black trousers that bunched around the top of his big black boots, and, despite the heat, he still had his long black coat on, open and hanging loosely at his sides. At least, Jake thought, he had left his hat in the car.

Jake and Billy were wearing t-shirts and shorts, but Billy's had a loose sketch of a woman's face, bright red lips, and the outline of a black hat pulled down and covering her eyes printed on the front. Jake's t-shirt was bright pastel green. Issy had a red floral bohemian-style mini dress on, and Amy had lowered her cat eye sunglasses and was staring at anyone who dared to look for too long.

To all those sitting outside the bar, it must have looked like a very unusual band had arrived.

"Seems we're causing quite a show," said Billy. "So much for doing things quietly. If that guy is in there he's going to know we're coming a mile off."

The Watchman agreed. "I'm going to head around the back," he said, intent on stopping anyone making a run for it.

"Let's go," Amy said, leading the way.

A table of guys called out as she got close to the front garden, suggesting she come sit with them, "And your blonde friend too."

Jake, Billy, and Issy were behind Amy and, therefore, hadn't seen the expression on her face, but they had seen the table quickly shut up and turn back to themselves, so they could guess.

Jake was just grateful she hadn't decided to take things further so early after their arrival. If Amy kicked off, the whole place would empty, and the Watchman couldn't stop all of them.

Jake sped up slightly and positioned himself on Amy's left flank in order to try and obscure her from as many people as possible.

Thankfully inside was even busier, and although they still received curious stares from those close to them, the music and bustle helped them get lost in the crowd.

"Okay. What now?" Issy asked, raising her voice above the music and chatter. "Should we split up?"

Billy and Jake automatically looked at Amy, who still looked like she was spoiling for a fight.

"No, I think it's best if we stay together," Billy said. "The Watchman's got the other side covered, let's head to the bar and maybe we can find a space to position ourselves. Then we start asking questions, slowly, and as subtly as we can. As soon as people here suspect we're looking for someone, they'll probably think we're undercover cops or something," he said.

As they shuffled by tables, and groups of people gathered, drinking, and talking loudly, the bass from the enormous speakers vibrated through them. Eventually they negotiated their way to the main, L-shaped bar. Issy spotted some free stools along the shorter side near the corner and made a beeline for them before anyone else settled there.

"Perfect," she said. "I guess we should order some drinks and try to blend in. Four beers?"

Billy and Jake nodded, perching on their stools, keeping an eye on Amy who appeared to be scanning the room for the Watchman.

"There he is," she said.

Issy got served quickly and handed out their beers. Amy took hers and drank without taking her eyes off the Watchman.

"That was fast," Billy said, looking over at the bar to see it was now mostly empty, and as good a time as any to start their enquiries. He walked around the corner of the L-shape and stood directly in front of the barman.

"This place is amazing," he said trying to sound as natural as he could. "Reminds me of this bar we used to go to up on the cliffs..." He faltered, pretending to have forgotten the name and hoping the barman would jump in.

But the barman didn't take the bait. "You from around here?" he asked.

"Me, no, but my mom moved out here when she split from my dad. I've been coming since I was a kid," Billy lied. "I've never been here before though."

The barman nodded thoughtfully. "Can I get you another beer or something?"

"How about something a bit stronger, and one for yourself. What rum have you got?" Billy asked, settling his elbows on the bar.

Jake was glad Billy had taken the initiative. "He's good at stuff like this," he said to Issy and Amy who were watching. "If that guy knows something then Billy's probably our best bet."

When Jake had been over in New York to visit, Billy had once taken him to a midtown dive bar to watch the Giants play the Philadelphia Eagles. He'd told Jake it was one of his favourite bars in Manhattan because it was out of the way, and less jumped up than the bars some of his Wall Street work friends went to. He had warned Jake it could get a little rough, but he said they would be fine.

The first thing Jake thought when he walked in was how big everyone was, and how small he felt in comparison. The place was more than *a little rough* and, judging by the atmosphere, the Eagles were already on top, even though the game had only just started.

Billy had muscled his way between a powerfully built man with a white moustache and beard in a sleeveless top, and a stoat-like man with black, receding hair wearing dark shades, despite the bar already being gloomy and, Jake was pretty sure, full of smoke.

Squeezing in Jake had reluctantly joined Billy at the bar, necking half his beer as soon as it arrived. The Giants were losing badly by half-time and the atmosphere soured further when a woman fizzed a beer bottle at the TV screen, which hit the corner of the frame and bounced off, smashing to the ground.

Jake had fully expected Billy to tell him to run, not to wait where he was while Billy made his way to the TV to talk to a bunch of angry drunks. If Jake had done that he was certain he'd have been punched and thrown out, but Billy had them mesmerised as soon as he opened his mouth. He told them it was a one off, the Giants ruled, and it was no big deal.

He invented a game on the spot, splitting the room into two teams and telling them they were going to bet. He made up a different bet every five minutes, some related to the game, like whether there would be a field goal or touchdown in that particular five minute spell, and some were bar-related like downing drinks and arm wrestling. After four or five rounds someone found a pack of cards, and then Billy simply started calling high or low. That kept everyone going until the game was over, by which point no one was interested in the score.

"Which would you recommend?" Billy asked the barman, after hearing their full rum selection.

The barman turned and reached for a particularly dusty looking bottle of English Harbour from the top shelf and poured two large measures.

"Try this," he said.

"Wow. That'll do it. Cheers." Billy clinked his glass to the Barman's and took a long gulp.

"Looks like the storm's here." The barman nodded in the direction of the door, watching the drinkers who had been at the tables and benches outside pile inside the main door to escape the rain.

Billy's heart sank. He was out of time.

"You know if that bar on the cliff's still going? Used to be one hell of a party," Billy fished, knowing he needed to speed things along.

The barman paused at first not understanding what he was talking about then he remembered how their conversation had started. "Yeh, it still goes, from time to time," he said.

"Kind of a sea theme, greens and blues, right?"

"Yeh, that's the one. Relaxed vibe, good music… it's Earl's place. He always makes sure it's well stocked too. Loves his rums."

Billy tried to hide the excitement from his voice. "Earl's place. He works here, right? Is he around?"

"Nah, not today. He's getting on, semi-retired I guess. That's why the cliff shack isn't open as often as it was. Hasn't done its reputation any harm mind, word travels fast around here and everyone knows, and everyone goes, when there's a party on," the barman said.

"Is he here?" Billy asked, knowing he was risking coming across too strong. Another flash of lightning crackled passed the windows and a clap of thunder boomed loud above the music, causing some people nearest the door to scream.

"Nah, he picks and chooses when he's in these days, and he isn't in tonight. Probably home with a bottle of this." He laughed, holding up the rum before replacing it on the shelf.

"He's got a place in Bolands?" Billy asked, casting his rod one last time before he went with a much more direct approach.

"He hasn't been there for a while. Moved out and bought a place, he's a couple of streets over that way now," he said, pointing. "Everyone knows where he lives because he's got this massive, awful-looking lime-green mailbox right out front."

"That's great, how much do I owe you?" Billy asked, reaching for his wallet.

"Uh, I dunno. Lemme check. Hold your horses man," the barman said, confused by Billy's change of pace.

"Actually, you know what? Don't worry about it, take this. It should cover it. Thanks, man," Billy said, hurriedly throwing down fifty U.S. dollars and leaving the barman stunned. He went to say something, but Billy had already turned back towards the others.

He walked back around the L-shaped bar, seeing Jake's eager face, knowing he must have been watching closely. He was just as excited to share his news, but before he got to them he froze, catching an unnatural jerky movement in the corner of his eye.

"Oh, shit," he said quietly, his eyes now following a large black-striped lizard creeping across the wall near the open window and heading in their direction.

Billy quickly checked the other walls, windows, and around the door, and immediately spotted two, then three more, all making their way over towards them.

He forced his body to move and ran back to Jake, Issy, Amy, and the Watchman, who'd found the others while Billy was at the bar.

"We need to get out of here, now!" Billy hissed, pulling Jake and Issy to their feet.

CHAPTER 36: NOWHERE TO RUN

"What is it? What's happened?" Jake asked.

But before Billy had time to answer Issy screamed so loud it hurt Billy's ears. He jumped and looked to see what had happened, expecting to find the lizards were much closer.

Instead, two heavy-looking weathered men with beards and tattoos had appeared in the doorway. One had a big coat on like the Watchman's but brown, and the other was wearing a black shirt, rolled up at the sleeves. He was pointing in their direction.

Before Billy could move he saw two more men stand up three tables back and over to his right from where they were, one bald and barrel-chested, the other had thick spiky black hair and was slightly taller and leaner, and seemed to be in command. He pushed drinkers and dancers out of the way, sending glasses and people flying, including two women wearing high heels who collapsed on the ground.

The bar turned in to chaos, men and women screaming over the music as they rushed for the exit.

A gunshot rang out, then another. Some of the melee threw themselves to the floor while others just kept pushing for a way out. Jake was first to locate where the shots had come from, pinpointing another storm hider at a back corner table, standing, his gun still smoking.

"Get down!" the Watchman yelled, pushing Issy and Jake to the ground, urging them to crawl behind the bar for cover.

Amy, meanwhile, stood perfectly still and assessed her options. She looked unaffected, despite the carnage ensuing around her. She tucked her loose hair behind her right ear and looked at the man who had fired at her, while he appeared to debate whether to wait a few more seconds for a clear shot, or to just start firing, and be damned. He decided to wait, as did Amy.

The lizards that had frozen when the gunshots blasted high in the air sprang back into action sensing the immediate danger was over.

One of the larger creatures, with a more meaty middle and bigger stripes than the others, took a chunk out of a man's arm as he fell back from the stampede near the exit. Blood surged from around his bicep and he screamed, his scream becoming even more shrill when he saw the bloated-looking reptile that had leapt from his arm to a nearby table and was readying itself for another attack.

* * *

The two men from the doorway were trying to force their way further inside towards where Jake, Issy, Billy, and Amy had been sitting, but the crowd still trying to escape in the opposite direction made their progress almost impossible.

In between trying to gain ground, and either avoiding the oncoming traffic or pushing people out of the way and to the floor as they approached, both men were angrily searching the area they'd last seen their targets, realising with frustration that they'd lost them.

All they could see now above and between the bobbing heads and flailing bodies, was an empty space where they *had* been. Their shipmate's idea to shoot his gun high into the air had been spontaneous, and extremely unhelpful.

The man with the brown coat stopped scanning the area when he found the dark-haired woman. He strained his eyes hard, disbelieving what he was seeing. She wasn't running, or screaming, or hiding, she was walking slowly forward, weaving around the tables and lingering crowd towards the shooter.

As he struggled to understand what she was doing, an ox of a man smashed him out of the way to get to the exit, winding him, and knocking him to the floor where he was kicked and trampled.

The man with the black shirt looked down to see his friend pull his arms and legs close to his body and cover his head with his arms before he was lost to the crowd. He thought about helping

189

but didn't want to give their target a chance to slip away, again. He'd seen what had happened to Leonard, and he didn't want the same fate.

* * *

Jake, Issy, and Billy huddled together pressing themselves up against the underside of the bar. Jake was on the left with Issy in the middle and Billy on the right, closest to the gap they'd found that had allowed them access.

All three of them were absolutely dripping with sweat. The storm was fully raging outside, but inside the heat, and still half the people, had yet to escape the building.

Billy wiped his brow with his forearm and blinked a few times to make sure he could see clearly, then risked crawling a few metres (a few feet) to the gap in the bar to see what was happening.

Directly in front of him, and all the way down the length of the room to where the shooter had been, was now practically empty. He looked over to his right and saw the remaining people forcing their way out, and a man lying face first on the floor just behind them, not moving. Perched on his back, their claws dug into his shoulder blades, were two of the lizards, one heavy looking and the other sinewy, feeding on different parts of him.

Billy just managed to swallow the sick that had lurched up in his throat at the sight and pulled himself together. He scanned the rest of the room, looking to the middle where he'd first seen the two men stand up a few tables back. They'd both been big guys, like soldiers. They were lying on the floor in widening dark pools of blood, both dead.

He quickly looked again across the restaurant for Amy and found her gliding towards the corner of the room where the shooter must be crouching behind an upturned table. Hope surged up in his chest as he began to believe they may actually make it out alive.

Based on the trail of bodies she'd already left behind her, he was pretty sure Amy wouldn't need any help, but he couldn't just watch. He stayed as low as he could and scrambled on all fours to the first table in front of him. He didn't know what he could do even if she did need his help, but he knew he had to be there in case she did.

Billy crouched behind a table leg and took quick short gasps of air. On the count of three he made another dash forward on all fours as fast as he could until he reached the next table. He looked to see where Amy was and saw she was still standing ahead of him, but he was closer, he had made up some ground.

He checked on the two storm hiders who'd been in the doorway, trying not to look at the body on the floor again. They were still there, but to his horror the people who'd been blocking their way had all but fled, and the lizards were on the corpse on their hind legs, looking over in his direction.

Billy surged forward again. His knees were hurting now on the hard floor, but he blocked it out, pushing harder and trying to propel his arms and knees faster along the ground.

He gained a few more yards before his left hand slipped on something wet. He fell forward, trying to catch the weight of his body with his right hand, but unable to stop his face hitting the floor, and his entire left side sliding through the sticky wetness.

He picked himself up quickly, searing pain behind his eyes. He touched his head where it had impacted and found it was wet too. Realising he was covered in blood he searched for the source, settling on the wide-eyed dead stare of a gruesome-looking bald man with tattoos staring back at him.

In a blind panic Billy tried to stand up so he could run, slamming his head hard into the underside of the table above him with a piercing crack that echoed through the now almost empty room.

* * *

Amy heard the noise even above the music still playing and spun on her heel, expecting to see another storm hider creeping up on her, only to find Billy in a pool of blood struggling to stay conscious underneath a table.

The shooter saw his chance. Thrusting himself upright and above the table he'd been using for cover, he aimed the gun point blank at the back of Amy's head.

Amy turned back just in time to see the shooter scream out in pain as the Watchman drove his dagger deep into his right thigh as he pulled the trigger.

The bullet skimmed past Amy's dark hair whipping it up in the air to the right of her face. She toppled over to her left crashing into a table and onto the floor not far in front of Billy, and the bullet continued on its way shattering one of the bottles above the bar behind her.

The Watchman, who'd been carefully making his way along the left-hand wall of the building undetected to the shooter's location ever since he fired, drove the dagger in to his victim's leg up to the hilt, before quickly pulling it out, and striking two more fatal blows.

Amy, stunned but otherwise unharmed, staggered angrily back to her feet, confused. She looked over to where the shooter had been and saw only the Watchman. She nodded in his direction, realising he'd saved her life then spun around to locate someone else to take her revenge out on, the noise of the bullet still ringing in her ear.

The Watchman retrieved his dagger and took a satisfied, and relieved, breath, knowing that had been his chance, and he'd taken it.

Billy looked up and saw Amy bearing down on him. He tried to stop heaving to save face, but his efforts just made him choke. He spat on the ground, wiped his mouth, and managed to hold his hand up feebly in an attempt to signal he was okay.

She shot passed him and began weaving in and out of the tables again, this time towards the doorway, knowing the Watchman was likely doing the same.

* * *

192

Having seen three of the other members in their group surprisingly disposed of, the man with the black shirt and the man with the brown coat had knocked over as many tables on their side of the room as they could to create some sort of barricade, and to obscure the visibility of their enemies.

The man in the long coat had stayed behind a table closest to the door, to prevent any of their targets sneaking out, and the man in the black shirt crawled and weaved between the tables, closing the distance in order to attack, just as Amy and the Watchman were doing but in the opposite direction.

He'd made it forward a few rows without incident but had run out of overturned tables to keep himself hidden and was wondering what to do. He risked a quick look around the side of his current location. He could see the pool of blood still spreading slowly across the floor, but he couldn't see any movement.

He felt uneasy. Before they'd left the ship the captain had briefed them on what they were facing, and what was expected of them. He'd told them not to be complacent, and that if any of them underestimated their enemy it would be their undoing, either at the hand of their target, or by the captain himself for their ineptitude.

The captain had never said *what* they needed to be so wary of, however. They knew about the Watchman, obviously, and they knew how difficult it was going to be to bring him down and were expecting some casualties.

But this dark-haired wild woman was something entirely different.

Rumours had been swirling aboard the Devil's Liberty that the Ghost had somehow sent for his protégé, and that they were just as emotionless and deadly as he had ever been.

He hadn't believed it, but as he crawled across the floor, the blood of his crew still spreading out in front of him, he began to think maybe the rumours had been true. He had seen the Ghost's handiwork and prayed he would never be on the receiving end.

Trying to force flashbacks of the Ghost from his mind, he took a deep breath, calmed his nerves and pushed on, his pistol in his right hand. Keeping as low to the ground as he could he hurried forward, only to find himself out of tables to hide behind and completely exposed. With nowhere obvious to hide he turned around quickly to check on his partner behind him. Just as he located him, still in position near the door, he saw Jake jump from his hiding place at the end of the bar, a rum bottle raised high above his head.

The bottle crashed down on the storm hider's nose knocking him to the ground, and the momentum from Jake's swing pulling him down on top of him.

The man in the black shirt hurried to help his friend who was fighting back, the blow enough to knock him down but not unconscious. He was much bigger than Jake and clearly gaining the upper hand as the two of them grappled in the doorway. Jake received a punch square and hard to the middle of his face and his head flew back and cracked on the wall behind him.

The man in the black shirt heard the noise. He was about to lurch forward when he felt the blade of the Watchman run across his throat, and collapsed in a heap, blood spurting from his neck.

The Watchman, and Amy who had joined him at his side, both looked towards Jake. They couldn't reach him in time. He was pinned to the wall, and one more blow to the head would likely prove fatal.

Amy reached for a glass on the table nearest to her and was about to hurl it through the air when Issy leaped out from behind the end of the bar and punched Jake's attacker on the back of the head.

As he fell back in surprise she thrust her right knee into his chin as hard as she could, her kneecap cracking on his skull making her scream in pain.

The man fell backwards, his head landing hard, and blood running into a pool where he lay.

CHAPTER 37: WOUNDED

Issy dragged herself over to Jake and cradled his head, searching for a pulse in his neck. Her knee was throbbing. Before she could find one his eyes flickered open and he groaned, reaching up to touch his right cheek which was already badly swollen.

"Oh thank God," Issy said, letting her head rest against the wall.

Billy slumped down next to them out of breath. "You both okay?" he managed.

"We're fine," Issy said, pausing to take a good look at him. "You, on the other hand, don't look so good," she said, attempting a smile.

Billy tried to wipe more of the blood off his face and clothes, the woman on his t-shirt was barely recognisable he had so much blood on him. He realised it was pointless and just gave both of them a hug being careful not to cause any more injuries.

He looked over his shoulder and saw Amy and the Watchman standing over the body of the man Jake had attacked, and Issy had finished off.

"Let's get out of here," Billy said. "The brother of the guy you found lives a few streets over. We can still finish this. Jake, Issy you okay to move?"

"I am, but Jake's had a pretty bad knock to the head," Issy said.

"There'll be more of them," said the Watchman, quick to remove the option of staying put. "We have to go, and fast."

"I'm fine," Jake said, trying to get to his feet and falling backwards straight away.

"Take it easy, man," Billy said, sliding Jake's arm around his shoulder and helping him to his feet.

Issy got herself upright and checked Jake's injuries. "This cheek's not too pretty, and there's a big lump at the back of his head, but he's not bleeding," she said gently.

"We need to get him to a hospital," Billy said.

Jake struggled in protest. "No, no way. We need to get what we came for, then we get out of here and I can get checked out. We did not come all this way for nothing," he said.

He wriggled free of Billy and was trying to make his way to the door, leaning on the wall for support. Issy and Billy knew it was futile trying to stop him, and if anything, it would put them in more danger.

"Okay, hold your horses," Billy said, catching up with him and slinging Jake's arm back around his shoulder, taking his weight.

"The barman said it's just a few streets up that way," Billy said, pointing over to the right as they stumbled out the doorway.

Outside was quiet, but none of them expected it to stay that way. Billy, Issy, and Jake knew the police must be on their way, and they didn't want to hang around to get questioned about the bodies inside, or the role each of them had played in them being there.

The Watchman and Amy were more wary about the rest of the storm hiders. The Watchman had said there would be more, and he was already at the gate of the outdoor seating area, crouched low to the ground, searching their surroundings for signs of another attack.

The rain didn't seem to bother him, he looked completely in his element as lightning crackled overhead, his hair wild and uncontrollable. He reminded Issy of when they'd first encountered him in similar surroundings in Barbados—and he'd come after them. She shuddered that they were now relying on him to help them get out of there alive.

Seeing nothing, the Watchman whistled loudly, using two fingers to signal to them to get moving.

Amy and Issy went first, with Billy propping up Jake just behind them, and the Watchman at the rear.

They stuck to the right-hand side of the road, the same side the bar was on, and whenever they could, they used the bushes, trees, and fences in front of the houses on that side as cover.

There was a slight incline heading up the road and the heavy rain meant water constantly washed passed them sloshing around their feet.

"This should be the one," Billy said, making sure everyone knew to stop. "Let's take a quick breather under those trees and then find the house." He scanned the area and spotted the green mailbox. "There. It's that one, about half way down the road."

He guided Jake to the dry patch underneath a cluster of large whitewood trees that had gathered on the corner at the end of the street. Amy, Issy, and the Watchman joined them, keeping an eye out for anything unusual.

Despite the weather worsening, the trees, which were particularly thick with many low hanging branches, provided an excellent shield to the majority of the wind and the rain.

"What's the plan? Who's going in first and what are we going to say?" Issy asked.

Amy and the Watchman looked like they simply wanted to break in, pin the man to the nearest wall, and interrogate him until they had what they came for.

"Let's try asking nicely first, okay?" Billy said, reading their looks. "Issy you still look the most respectable, you should go first and knock on the door, with us just behind you."

"I'm covered in blood!" she declared, before looking at the state of the rest of them. "Okay, sure. Maybe I can tell them we were in a car accident and we need to use their phone or something."

"Sure, that'll do. We just need to get out of danger and in a position to talk to this guy, hopefully he'll just tell us which way the anchor was pointed and then we can get the hell out of here," Billy said, before adding, "Oh, shit." As movement from one of the branches overhead caught his attention.

The others looked up in to the trees, at first not seeing anything, then Issy screamed.

Three striped lizards were slinking their way ever so slowly down through the branches above them, darted forward sensing they'd been discovered.

They were smaller than the ones Billy had seen inside the bar, thinner, and nimbler. They reminded him of snakes with legs. The first of the creatures reached its launch point, taking off from the tip of a branch near Jake's head. It flew through the air straight at him, rows of tiny sharp teeth bared, when Amy plucked it clean out of the air with one hand, gripping around its middle.

She brought its hissing mouth close to her eyes and squeezed, watching as its expression changed from anger and frustration to shock and pain, and finally nothing. Amy flung the carcass of the lizard down on the sodden ground and searched for the next one.

The skinniest of the three was next in line but just managed to claw the branch it was scurrying along hard enough to bring itself to an ungainly halt, having seen what had happened to its friend. The third lizard had perched itself high out of reach, hissing down upon the scene below. Amy made sure the skinny lizard closest to them fled before turning away, certain they were no longer a threat, for now.

Issy, Billy, and Jake had become so used to Amy in her new form they weren't even that surprised by her sudden violent outburst and were just grateful she was on their side.

Even Issy no longer felt quite as protective. Her main goal now was to stick close and help bring back the Amy she knew, just as soon as she figured out how to do that.

"Time to move," the Watchman said, sidling out of the shelter of the trees, and not taking his eyes off the opposite side of the road.

"What is it?" asked Jake, peering out of their hiding place in the direction the Watchman was looking.

"Over there," Billy pointed. First one, then two storm hiders appeared from the inside of a rundown house with pale red walls, then another three behind them. They had a short gathering, said a few words, then started marching towards Billy and the others, more than one carrying a gun.

"Get to the house. Run!" Amy commanded, walking out in to the road to join the Watchman and block the way of the five advancing storm hiders.

"What? No! I'm not leaving you out here, you can't—"

"GO!" Amy bellowed, cutting her off.

Issy turned and joined the others.

"Come on, don't worry she's got this. Let's get the directions," Jake said, taking her by the arm.

Issy looked back one last time to see two of the storm hiders raise their arms and fire. She spun her head back around in fear, running for her life, expecting to feel a bullet blast its way through her back.

CHAPTER 38: THE LAST STAND

As the first storm hiders had fired, Amy had darted to the left and the Watchman to the right, hoping to cause at least a few moments of indecision for their enemies.

The bullets had flown narrowly wide of their marks, but the other three attackers were ready to fire another volley, and Amy and the Watchman both knew they needed to find some cover then get in close if they were to stand a chance.

He looked up ahead and saw a white Rav4 parked up on the kerb. In a few long strides he made it to within a metre (three feet) of the vehicle and slid the rest of the way through the wet river of water that was running underneath the car's tyres and along the road.

He pulled his feet in right before a bullet clipped the bumper, and another whistled just wide. Then another bullet buried itself into the side of the car, and another, and another.

The Watchman edged his way around quickly, so the Toyota was between him and the three men pursuing him as they continued to fire.

Wanting to see how close they were he pressed his back to the side of the car and slid to the front in a squat position. He was about to poke his head out a fraction when another bullet flew just over the top of the bonnet, and over his head. The Watchman slammed himself back into position, trying to figure out his next move.

He was penned in, and they were closing fast. They could sense the kill.

His only hope was that Amy, with the help of the Ghost, was fairing a lot better.

CHAPTER 39: MUTINY

The more time the Ghost had spent inside Amy's head the deeper he'd been able to burrow into her subconscious and steal control.

He'd been mostly satisfied with his progress, seeing the fight through her eyes, and leading her and her friends towards him.

There had been a few close calls, and he'd nearly ripped the big American's head clean off for distracting him, and almost costing the life of his host and only hope of escape, but it had revealed more about the Watchman's intentions.

The Ghost knew now he was no longer with the captain, and he'd obviously figured out the Ghost was pulling Amy's strings. Whether the Watchman could be fully trusted or not was inconsequential, without him the Ghost would be back on his island with no way out. He owed him; he knew that.

Through Amy's eyes he could see, on the opposite side of the street, the white Toyota Rav4 was now riddled with bullet holes. Three of the captain's men were running forward, surrounding the Watchman, who he knew was taking cover on the other side of the battered vehicle.

A few metres (few feet) away from Amy's hiding place two of Captain Sands' best men were closing in too, both with their guns trained on the black BMW, the only car on her side of the street.

The Ghost knew Amy had no weapon, and he couldn't see anything within reach that she could use, her bare hands would have to do.

He was confident he could get Amy to take care of the two men almost upon her, but no matter how he played out events in his head all outcomes resulted in the Watchman's death. Half an hour earlier he might have seen that outcome as an upside; now he had a debt to repay.

Suddenly he remembered something. The Watchman had said the gods were at odds with each other and not all of them backed the captain any longer. He didn't know why the thought had occurred to him, but he sensed it could be useful and tried to force it to become clearer.

Then he had it. Allowing Amy and her friends to get this close to their hidden islands had angered them, not all of them believed Sands' army was fit for purpose anymore.

They're divided.

The land hadn't swayed, the lizards were proof of that, and the sea god was of no use to the Ghost now.

He looked up at the storm through Amy's eyes, ignoring the gunshots across the street, and the men one step away from the car.

Summoning all his energy he focussed on the clouds above him, staring into the wind and the rain, putting himself amongst the thunder and lightning.

He promised to rid the Caribbean of Sands and his men, and protect the hidden islands, if they would just help him get free.

He's failed you, but I won't.

Just as Sands' men leapt behind the BMW ready to fire, lightning tore out of the sky overhead and connected with the tops of both men's scalps, lifting them off the ground and setting them alight as electricity surged through their veins. It vanished as quickly as it had appeared dropping them to the ground in a smoking heap.

Amy got to her feet and looked over to the Watchman just in time to see the three men that had surrounded him light up in exactly the same manner.

She looked around herself at the devastation and smiled.

As the thunder faded away all that was left was the sound of the rain still bouncing off the bonnets of the bullet-riddled cars.

Amy went to see if the Watchman was still alive.

Stepping over the smouldering bodies she found him kneeling, his back against the car. He looked up at Amy's face as she pulled him to his feet and saw the Ghost's blazing eyes staring back at him.

He didn't know exactly what had just happened, but he had a strong sense war had begun.

CHAPTER 40: DIRECTION

Issy looked through the window into the street. A blinding flash lingered, before outside became black again.

Worrying about what might be happening to Amy she pressed on with her questioning of the elderly man sat in his lounge chair in front of her.

"Earl, thanks again for inviting us in. We'd never driven in weather quite like this and we just lost control of the car and it spun. I don't really know what happened, but we got out and, we made it here."

"Mmhmm," was all Earl replied, picking up his glass of neat rum and taking a sip. The barman had been right about how Earl liked to spend his days off.

"Well, anyway, thank you," Issy stammered, positive he didn't believe her and unsure how to get to the point.

"The thing is, we were looking for something, before we crashed I mean," she started.

Earl didn't move a muscle, just sat calmly waiting for Issy to continue.

"We read about this amazing bar on a cliff here, in Antigua, and… oh, this is ridiculous." She sighed impatiently, horrific images of Amy lying dead outside in the rain flashing through her head.

"We came here looking for an anchor, and we found it, but it wasn't where it was supposed to be, it was hanging above the bar in the shack on the cliff… and we need to know where it was pointing before it got there," she said shakily.

Earl blinked a few times, then took another sip from his drink.

"We were told you put the anchor in the bar Earl, where did you find it?" she asked, trying desperately to hurry him along.

Earl studied the two men behind her.

"We don't mean to cause any distress," Jake said quickly.

Earl laughed, a deep, croaky laugh. "You have no idea what you're into," he muttered.

Apparently satisfied with Jake's response he got up and faced the window. Outside remained completely black with no further flashes of lightning, and there were no more deafening claps of thunder or gunshots, only the sound of the heavy rain that was still falling remained.

"I knew someone would come, eventually," he said. "I wasn't sure I'd still be alive to see it, but here you are," he stated, turning back around to face them.

Issy looked to the others to see if they knew what he was talking about, but Billy and Jake were just as confused.

"We knew when we found it, it was important. You could just feel it," Earl continued. "I was with my brother, we were on watch that day, up on the cliffs, looking for *them*."

"Who were you looking for?" asked Jake, getting excited. He suspected he knew the answer but wanted Earl to confirm his thoughts out loud.

"Storm hiders. We were using the trail to keep watch. Any sightings and we were to report back, and if the sightings were close, or looked particularly threatening, we were to raise the alarm," Earl said.

"You are part of the resistance, just like Nicolas," Jake said.

Earl nodded, pleased they were now passed the game-playing stage.

"They've been terrorising the islands for centuries, and for such a long time we've been helpless against their attacks... until recently. Something's happening." He waved at the dark window behind him and the rain still streaming down the glass.

"Sightings of them have become more frequent, at sea and on land, and more of them are dying too, it's not just us anymore. It's empowered us, made us believe it's time," he said.

"Time for what?" Issy asked him slowly.

"Time to rise up and fight," Earl said, spit escaping from his lips.

"Whatever you're looking for, I'm guessing it's part of all this. And if you're not with them, it sure seems like they're going to some lengths to stop you," he said, looking at the blood still caked to Billy's face and clothes and Jake's now grotesquely swollen cheek.

"Which is why I'm going to tell you…" He let his words hang in the air.

Billy, Jake, and Issy held their breath, praying he'd just spit it out.

"We found the anchor buried in the side of the cliff, my brother Barnabas tripped and fell, I thought he'd tumbled all the way to the bottom and was a goner. But he'd hit some sort of ledge.

"I reached down to pull him up, but he was shouting at me to come down. It took me a while to truly believe that's what he was asking of me, but when I let the words sink in finally I scrambled down to his location to see what he was yelling about.

"There was a hole in the side of the cliff, kind of like an animal's burrow, but something big. We managed to crawl inside. He wanted me to go first, you won't believe it to look at me now, but I was the smaller one," he said, grinning and patting his belly.

"Anyway, inside there was a space like a small cave. The roof was only a couple of metres (a couple feet) off the ground but it went back maybe three or four metres (ten to thirteen feet) and was about the same wide… and we found the anchor dug into the ground, pointing out to sea."

"Do you remember exactly where you found it, and where it was pointed?" Jake asked eagerly.

"Of course. As I said, we knew it was important. We kept a record of everything but decided that we couldn't leave it there. We knew storm hiders were using the trail at that point, and if we stumbled across it, then so would they. Whatever it led to, we didn't think they knew about it, and we didn't want them to have it.

"We carefully excavated the site, making sure we weren't seen when we were working, four of us at a time. Two to dig and two lookouts.

"We decided, in the end, it was best hidden in plain sight... it was my brother's idea. And that's why we attached it to the wall above the bar. As you've seen the anchor is only a small one, around a metre-and-a-half (almost five feet) long, so it wasn't too difficult to hang it, and we figured that anyone who saw it would think, 'Hey, nice decoration,' and that would be that.

"We thought that by removing it from its hiding place, we'd remove the context, and no one would think there was anything more to it. Only we'd know, and we'd take that secret to our graves.

"Unless someone came looking, someone other than them," he added.

Issy couldn't take it any longer. "My friend's out there, with *them*. I have to go and help her," she said, getting up and rushing to the door, annoyed she'd stayed listening for this long.

She pushed passed Billy and Jake before they could stop her, but as she reached for the handle the door flew open and Amy, soaking wet, was standing there with the Watchman behind her.

Issy flung herself at her friend, ignoring her eyes, which had become darker and even more disturbing than when she'd last seen her.

She dragged Amy inside, and the Watchman followed, shutting out the wind and rain behind them.

Earl visibly recoiled a little but recovered his composure quickly, studying the two strangers who'd appeared in his home.

"Friends of yours?" he asked Jake, looking for confirmation he was safe to continue. Jake nodded.

Earl sat back in his seat and took another sip of his rum. He came to the conclusion they must, for now, all be on the same side, including the storm hider, and whatever the wild woman was—otherwise they would surely all be dead.

"Pass me that book," Earl said, making his mind up and pointing to a hardback on his coffee table.

Jake forgot the pain in his face and located the book and handed it to Earl, his chest pounding.

Earl flicked through the pages until he found the right one, then placed it back on the table, now open at a specific page. Even from a distance they could see it was a map of the Caribbean.

In clear red ink, running from the south west coast of Antigua, past Monserrat, and out in to the Caribbean Sea was a sharp red line, marking the direction the anchor had been facing.

Billy quickly took a picture with his phone, scared the book would suddenly disappear. He looked at Jake and knew his friend was already drawing on the line from the anchor they'd found in Barbados in his mind to locate the point the two lines crossed.

"We did it," he whispered under his breath, gripping Billy's shoulder and grinning at Issy. He looked at Amy, wanting to share the moment with her too, but her head was down, and she was still staring hard at the map, lost in thought.

"Thank you, Earl," Jake said full of emotion, taking the old man's hand and pressing firmly. He wanted to say more, but his mind flooded with the possibilities that now lay ahead. Overwhelmed he just smiled and stared at the point on the red line he now knew the hidden islands to be, still unable to believe they'd found them.

"You be careful now," Earl said seriously, looking at each of them.

But Amy wasn't listening, she couldn't. The Ghost had pushed her to the side and was staring, transfixed, at the line on the map—he'd waited a long time for this.

Behind his vision of the book in front of him he could see lightning flashing over the top of trees, and he heard the screeching of the wild birds as they flocked to his island.

The Watchman had been right, war was coming, and once the undisturbed islands were unleashed upon the world there would be more than just men and gods to worry about.

He took stock of the room. He'd been surprised by Billy, Issy, and Jake. They had shown remarkable doggedness and resilience after he dismissed them off the bat. The Watchman had also proven himself on more than one occasion, even saving the woman's life to keep his hopes of freedom alive. Without him the Ghost wouldn't have made it this far.

He was satisfied they were even now, though, after what had happened on the road outside. The Ghost didn't owe him anything, and he preferred it that way if he was going to keep him around too.

He looked again at the map.

They just needed to get there, and fast. He couldn't afford to give Sands another opportunity to stop him.

"We're going to need a boat," Jake said, thinking aloud and on the same wavelength.

Amy smiled. "I know just where to get one."

THE END

A Few Words

Thank you for reading. I hope you enjoyed it! It would be greatly appreciated if you could leave a short, honest review on the site you purchased this book.

Book 3 of The Undisturbed Islands Trilogy, Caribbean Ghosts, is now available on Amazon, as is book 1, Rum Country, if you haven't read it yet.

For more Caribbean adventures and news of upcoming novels, follow me on Instagram @jwilliamauthor

Printed in Great Britain
by Amazon